Citi

Other books by RA Washington:

Citi

a novel by RA Washington

red giant books

There were hints before you cut.
The things we unravel when strained,
it seems as if we do not know anything
beyond moves to placate the suffering
    You.

                —Character of a Far Away novel.

MOUF.

I wish to commit a murder. The rub is that I am also a coward. I am more comfortable with a slow self-rubbing-out.

The she and he of this is informed by denial. Plain. Simple.
The lies we tell, the tiny cuts we create—inflict.
There is a certain malice to knowing, of course; but I am done placing myself along the center. There will be no more I.
That is western, and the west has failed me, and perhaps has failed a few of you. Do not be alarmed, this is not an attempt at vengeance, this is not subversive. We will not deem ourselves clever enough, nor do we have the courage to do anything that would alter how you view yours, and how you will die clutching what you thought even though there will be a life's work of evidence that you were mistaken.

Yes, I wish to commit a murder, and yes, I plan on telling you how it could, well, will occur.

You are sitting in tall August grass, the sun is just so across your face. At six, perhaps younger, red innocence hinting your cheeks. A while ago I found you, slipping your woman's work in a copybook. Every failed attempt of a man to cheek coupling. I guess the orgasm is still mist. I'm learning to not hold out. Even though it scares me, and when afraid my maleness overwhelms intent. Then I hide in the folds of magazines, the glossy tit or thigh, wishing my body was not so monster, that just once I could seduce with a look—no words or tongue.

Before I found myself without a MOUF, slipping in first person and falling in third, the narrator annoyed at not being able to pin me down. Narrators are funny about this.

Perhaps I am formerly of family. Perhaps a disaster has occurred that left me without speech, left us without CITI. As far as I have been, and in spite of all the WE is said to be.

[**Before, Before**]

SHE: Do you think you will be home early? I miss you.

HE: I will try. We have a huge project coming down. You do know that I love you?

SHE: I do know, but there is more to it than saying so.

and perhaps the narrator is a man, and decides to speak to her inner life.

SHE was always this way. Pushing HIM to connect, wishing for the connection of the silver screen, the embrace of a HIM, or THEM. For the most part HE did, SHE was HIS savior, and SHE was HIS death. HE feared HER. So warm. So present. Unlike any woman HE had ever known.

The home they made—memory pixels shake loose, the timeline is fraying; the how WE got here, and how THEY will end, and the where SHE has gone.

The utters. Just grunts along the scars.

[**Begin**]

His whole of him ached like a battlefield, the aftermath smolder was present in his face. His mouth was cracked by wind, but all of this happened long ago, the wound, a separate mouth turned on its side. He tried to gather moisture in the caked destroyed whole, but spit had left him long ago.

The long ago—he fought the urge to scream but what he could not control through a command from his brain, he snuffed with his hands over the wound. The middle night, that time, hours before dawn, was the darkest in the deserted Citi. He still blinked to make his eyes adjust to the darkness. It was a habit; it was as useless as praying.

Had there been a Citi here? He remembered it destroyed. He remembered it killing him. The day-to-day. The knowing had left him a long time ago. He walked using the old highway. No sound. Not even the wind spoke. He could actually see himself slipping, the real and the lie. The time and its end.

From time to time in this we will let each other speak. We will depend on each other. This story we have, caught in the mouths of animals. The barely alive suffer too; and we kill, and we miss, but the missing is another story, for a different book.

Even though he could no longer see he thumbed at a fraying snapshot. We do not know of who, and he cannot see it. He thinks there is light further toward what looks like a slope. He blinks more, and stops himself from having the thought that he is no longer a man, more beast, he attempts to utter the word: 'B-E-A-S-T' but stops at 'B-E'

There was a life before this. Someone had loved him—they made a child out of this, and later another. He could not remember his children's names; one day he reached for them and they were gone. He tried for what seemed like hours, but it was only minutes to remember how to kill oneself. He could not, so he existed within the flesh of misery alone and failing. Grunts replaced words. Clawing replaced the fine motor skill of telling time. He knew it had not been hours, it could have been days, months, even years. A face does not disintegrate in hours. For us it is just minutes.

What he knew:

No longer felt the tiny and naturally sharp rocks, stones, pebbles on which he lay. He no longer cared what he ate. He did not know warmth. It felt like a lifetime of not remembering, of not seeing another human being, and all of this, contradicted the new nightmare of seeing her face.

It started to hover an inch off his pupil. This beginning. I will not feign to not be affected by what I tell you. It is impossible to be present in this and detached. For this is how we arrive at autumnal CITI, its population disbelief, its buildings struck with man's ability to justify suicide.

I wander these hills looking for my face. I am not willing to disappear like this CITI, and I am sure that I have. It is not for me to decide. For a second I thought I had seen someone, a shadow running along the burnt brush. I chased, and then lost the shadow against the backlit rim of the sun. Now I am taking the road back the way I came, hoping there is something that I missed—that escapes, that lives.

I want to imagine them all. My wife watching me sleep, her hand against my side. Her fingers are always warm, she pulses her intent. I am safe here. Lust allows me to create her, I know it is not the real her, but I am a man so delusion lets me believe that I can create a face, a body. I idle and touch myself. There is no wind, there is no one so it is becoming my only tether to a here.

The children are harder. I do not know them. I do not need them. They are holes in my manhood. She was them, she kept them real for me, it was our contract. I let them laugh in my head, they are close enough in age to be like twins. A boy, a girl. I name them each step, only to forget the next, this wander. This is not real. How many days before I can see again, taste again. The air smells of charred metal. So thick you reach out, feel it. I scoop at it, because it is getting in my eyes. It is choking my throat.

I slide down the broken side of the highway trying not to tumble or cut my hands more than they already are. At the bottom is smoke, it smells like someone cooking, but I cannot tell from what direction so I circle back toward the highway, try to pick up the scent again. It is stronger the closer I get, but there are no structures, no fire. How am I smelling cooking? My mind plays at hunger.

There along the high ridge, I can see a figure. Slim, arms flail—I scramble down and call out. It comes out as a grunt and a longer utter emote.

"Hey who's there? Don't come any closer, I don't have anything for you."

I say what I think is 'I'm just hungry', but it sounds like 'ugh, huh.

"What's wrong with you? I don't understand."

I scramble down the bank, and she meets me, a large knife in my face,
"What do you want, where did you…"

I point. I have no use for words, words are now my enemy.
"Do you want to eat? Why can't you talk?"

I try to look at her face, but her knife is all I see.
"Come over, but don't try anything. I will kill you."

She moves quickly back to her fire, she places what looks like bread on a slab of rock, and then a chewed cup of liquid. It smells great, I get dizzy from it, how long had it been since I had eaten.

"I've been here for weeks, have not seen a soul. Eat, relax. Just don't try anything."

I nod, and I slurp down the broth. It is too hot, but I don't care, it burns and I try to slow down by wiping my mouth with the back of my hand.

"You want more? Here, have some more. My name is Lise."
She extends her hand, I take it, the palm is rough, the tips of her fingers are calloused chunks, warm.
"Where did you wander off from?"

I go to speak, and again just grunts.
"What happened to your mouth? Does it hurt?"
I nod no.

She reaches up to touch it and I scramble back.
"I'm not trying to hurt you, let me see. Oh, its just scabs, you need to wash it off."

Lise comes back with the ends of a rag and washes my face.
"There. There. When was the last time you washed up?"

I slurp, and slurp more broth.
"I woke up down here, I don't know when I came, or how. I remember being at a dinner with my… and then light. Lots of light. Explosions, people screaming. Sirens. Then darkness. Like the whole sky was a small room, and you could flick a switch. It took weeks before my eyes adjusted. Haven't seen anyone, haven't seen any animals, birds. I found this bread a couple of days ago. Cut the moldy parts. Found some supplies."

She points,
"Over past the ridge, near that far tree line."
I nod.

"Do you remember anything? Right. You can't speak."
I blink.
"You are welcome over here by the fire. I just need to gather more wood. I was thinking of walking back up the bank toward the highway, and trying to find some people, but there is water here, and some cover so I don't know if I should. Would you go with me? It would be better to travel with you than alone."
I nod.

And then go for more wood. As I walk I can feel her eyes on me, it feels familiar. I can see that face that haunts me again, then it fades. My face is wet, and it takes me a moment to realize I have been crying.

As I come back with more firewood, I can see her back, bare against the fire's light.

"Hey I'm just washing up, it's okay. I don't care if you see me. It's nice to be seen don't you think?"

I pile the firewood against some rocks. It seems as though everything makes sense in her little camp, the firewood even has a place. I sit down and place some branches onto the fire. The sparks glint.

"I wish you could tell me your name. Where you are from. How you got that wound."

She is dressed again, and says,
"It's important to have a routine, to pretend that it is the way it was, that none of this has happened."
I nod.

Lise looks right at me, her eyes trained as if she is willing me to speak. She reaches out and places her hands along my wound, she lets her finger trace the scar, she takes my hand, and places it against her left breast. Her heart is the loudest sound I can hear. I let my fingers pulse against, seeking nipple, I linger there, my middle finger rubbing back and forth against the bud.

We lay facing. Her right hand on my face, my right on her breast. We lay as the fire dies to smolder. Each of us trying to trace through dreams the how we got here, the what we lost, the what is left. I close my eyes to the light of a rising sun, the red rim puckered against the horizon. The lump in my throat is massive, choking me, she is asleep, slumped against my side as if it has always been her, me.

"You wish to know me?"
I hear the last words through the haze of sleep. She is up, I can hear the fallen leaves under foot.
"We should pretend this is what we know."

I am up now, the drool on my chin from the hard sleep. She comes very close, I sit up and trying to sound a word, my face twists, but she understands and reaches out.

"It is fine, there is no reason to force it. As your scar heals you will talk again. Look, I think we should walk down toward the highway side, toward the Citi, see if we can figure out where everyone is, and if we don't see anything, we can always come back here. I've been thinking about doing it, but now that you are here, I'm not scared. You would protect me right?"
I nod.
"You seem like you would. You seem like the type. You think of yourself as a good person don't you?"
This time I don't nod.

PRESENT TIME

We keep looking for the beginning, but thinking better of it in the hope that (you too wish for a gone?)

I'm waiting for Cushmere, the TV is on, chain smoke. There are pages, but they are shit, full of sentiment and spit. It has been 96 days since my last erection.

I am failing at my male privilege, and it is showing. I cannot even dominate my own penis, my inert sense is that I should cut a vein, and pour my smoke in and shrug against the vague hope of me dying. The TV is on, infomercial for the new self help tape by the foremost moral leader of Black America, the darling of this supposedly post-racial age: Rev. Dr. Dozier E. Pennyworthy. In the 30 minute infoset, he is hocking a product that can save young girls from the pervasive pressure of Feminism, to re-establish the true Christian hierarchy of God, the Father, God, the Son, and in possession of the holiest of Ghosts. The head of a blessed family is the GUY, or THE DUDE. The patriarch who commands all of the vaginas that exist within the home with a firm and utterly deviant sexual molestation in order to keep said vaginas pure, ands in the service of God, and the Church.

TV.
Young woman, knee length skirt, long sleeved blouse. She is in a very conservative heel, facing camera, and by proxy me (us) the viewer.
She starts,

"Father says it is important to always be presentable, even when you don't feel like it. I just listen and do what Father says because it is easier that way, besides I do enjoy it when Father's friends come over and he asks me to twirl around real fast for them. I feel free when I get going, I twirl faster and faster till I can almost feel myself being lifted up. When I first twirled I was worried that Father's friends would think bad of him if my undergarments showed, but he told me not to worry. That was part of what made it so cute, and pretty soon it was a hit at any party Father threw."

TV.
screen cuts to a montage of the young woman doing housework, her apron just so, her hair catching the light from the gleaming windows.

"It is very important to listen to your fathers no matter what, even if you have to sit on some gross man's lap, it is not for you to understand your father's plan for you. You just have to play your roll. Sometimes the men get excited by the party, and stuff and they prick me a bit, but it is okay, Father says it is natural for boys to get excited that way. It is what girls were put on God's earth to do."

At the end of the infomercial, some 60 young women, of all races and shapes, the demure, the plump, join the good Rev. Dr. on stage, as he turns in a slow Tyrone Powers full tooth smile at the camera and says,

"You too can control your household and make your daughter the Christian weapons they should be. You too can prep them for a healthy life and future domestic violence within the holy institution of marriage. *These liberals want you to believe that it is not your right to be in service of yourself, but this is how we have become so diseased, so malnourished, so far away from God's true intention PRAISE JESUS. It will start, the rebuilding of our America will start with the daughters, and their anointed wombs, trained at your anointed hand!"*

Cushmere came over with some hash candy, and a copy of Spike Lee's *OLDBOY* remake. I forgive him the flick choice because he brought drugs, and although Cushmere likes to play a bit of the Black Nationalist, he really is just a conflicted suburban mix-breed with questionable taste. I think his politics are informed mainly by his love for 90s Hip Hop and his homo-erotic fascination with Franz Fanon.

Plus he may feel a bit guilty because his parents were able to cash in on the Jesus-led Affirmative Action of the 70s so they could afford to offer the sort of protection that allows children to try on identities in the culture lore. When I met him he was straight edge, and only listened to Minor Threat.

When I asked him after few shared joints why no Bad Brains he looked over his thick black frames, which were really just as dense as the end of a glass bottle of Mexican Coca-Cola and whispered in his best Debbie Harry:

"It's a bit predictable given my hue don't you think?"

A brilliant retort when one is 19, but severely edging along stupidity when said at 40.

[I apologize for starting here
it's not that I wish to destroy the concept of narrative.
but calmer and less modern,
and predictably more male folks
have mastered it.
now their doughy red and white

pasty faces are alight on
the high tower of the student
debt machine. these literature
buffs who have read everything
(except Guy Debord) and now
serve me coffee.]

So Cush comes over, and we sit :

Cush: Look B, i'm not exactly sure the candy is safe. My first patch
gave me toddler shits, and I was blind for at least five hours.

Me: So give me a piece. I've always wanted to be Ray Charles.

The recipe is taken from the Arab Kif Candy.
A cup of finely diced almonds.
a clove of ginger.
nutmeg. (large amount, but to taste.)
Brown sugar.
and of course, DRUGS.
Mix it into a gummy paste and bake. (45 mins at 300)

You can then place the baked paste on crackers or bread, or just
pop it in your mouf. The effects are very similar to weed cookies,
the tinge of twinks along your MOUF, then the body buzz, and,
if you are the type:
colors!

and finally revelations: you see yourself as a Shaman, a seer, it is good for the esteem, But, ultimately such things are worthless.

Cush: I was recalling Heather. Do you remember her?
he does not wait for me to answer.
didn't she die? I seem to remember her dying. I miss her.

Me: She is not dead. She just doesn't speak to anyone. She is a re-born christian, plus I would of run away from you too.

Cush: What the fuck does that even mean? Most of my bad habits I learned from you.

Me: Well let's see: the constant depression, the insistence that you possess superhuman abilities, the lazy no job, no ambition. I think you may have had those traits way before we started hanging.

Cush: You act as if its a bad thing. I for one tend to think that any striving will only lead to disappointment, and further brain-washing in the service of Patriotic Fervor; like rooting for the home team and shit like that.
(I watch him take his 4th cigarette from my pack.)

Me: OK, lets suppose that you are right, what does any of that have to do with your habit of tying women up in your apartment while you read Blake and rub your tiny male member on their faces. Or that butt plug trick that you reveal on the first date?

Cush: If a woman cannot understand why anyone would feel pleasure from self taint stimulation then she may not be human.

Me: Replicants are perfect copies of us. you happen to be such a navel gazing fucker that i doubt you could even detect one if they existed for real. but i am impressed that in all the years i've known you, you always manage to bring up Blade Runner.

Cush: That is not even impressive. I suspect you may be pulling my chain a bit, but I think you should help me look her up so I can apologize. She was the one.

Me: Let it go. there is no way she would even talk to either one of us ever again. i'm amused by the whole idea. lets pretend we did find her, what would you say?
(more candy, body buzz)

He stands and bolts for the bathroom, I hear grunts so I turn up the movie. Cush emerges 25 minutes later.

Cush: Perhaps I have eaten too much of the hash.

Me: Well at least it didn't happen while you were riding back to your place. I still want to play our little game. What would you say to her if we were to get in touch?

Cush: Come on man, fuck that. Its a crazy idea. I have nothing to say, there is not a sincere bone in my body. I'm a charlatan.

Me: So you've been reading Paul Bowles again? Say no more. Such a big faker.

Cush: Do you mind if I make some tea?

Me: Come on, what would you say?

Cush: I'm going to make some tea, and when I get back you better not still be an asshole.

****

CUSHMERE leaves around 3 AM, and I'm sitting in my living room looking out of the window. I have seen six cop cars in 20 minutes; although none of them seemed to be interested in doing anything about the two white boys attempting to buy crack off this burnt looking crackhead named Minnie who keeps time over this way. It's not warm enough to have the window open but I can imagine what's being said:

Minnie: Get yo' lil' asses out of here, like I can help yo' stupid ass. WHAT?
Can I help you find some rock? Are you boys lost? Let me borrow some money.

WHITEboyONE: Fuck you bitch!

WHITEboyTWO: What the fuck you talking about bitch? We will fuck you up.

Minnie: I'm gonna count to ten and then I'm going to kill you. TEN.

And the Minnie pulls out the biggest handgun I've ever seen from out of no where, and shoots both of the boys in their dicks. The gun disappears as fast as it appeared and a few seconds, wait, minutes later a patrol car rolls up, carrying Flatends, and Jobson opens the trunk and thuds their corpses into the car. Minnie pulls her crackhead face off and reveals the metal casing, points up to my window and:

I
COME
TO.
My body splayed all over my floor, clothes still on. There is vomit caked to my face, it has dried my eyes shut. I stagger up and go to the sink. No water. I go to the bathroom, turn knobs, NO WATER.

"What the fuck!"

I place my face in the toilet bowl, and hope that I finally wake up, this was nothing more than me having a low tolerance for sugared debauchery.

***JUDGEMENT is the reward for having loved someone. It seeps in, often before either person is aware. The familiar play of cutting each other.

What we want, and what we need becoming a confusion in the set pieces. The opposite of an acceptance, the reverse of a care.

I am in the throes of a crisis, but I'm hopeful that I will be able to drink my way out of it. I've wanted to be cum-spent in the arms of a girl, as if the sheer youth of her, the budding envelope, the flick, nip when taken by veteran hands, and in this I could be remade. cocksure, ready.

I wish for the time when I could slam my cock into dry wall, the erection is the totem, it is supreme maleness. Before, Before. When she expected me to be an upright, without the disposition of a giant coward head—
pretending to think, to be. Only to realize that I was dead, and had been a corpse for sometime. The rub being a bit more like a cold bucket of water. Or the vague wantings of a retarded child. MUTE, BLIND, DEAF.

The phone rings. I do not answer for I am busy hiding myself underneath a blanket, my little fort. My abuse.

Walking now, dusk. Recalling how I first conceived of a murder. It could be totally random, a stranger. Dark. Walk up behind and the blade slow thrust. Let it simmer. Let dig. Blood, just a trickle, the seconds would melt as I held it there. The wound growing. The pull, the spirit. I would watch the fear creep along the sides of their eye, mouth slack. The blade wiped clean. And then I would be taken up, like in rapture, up. My body falling away, spirit release like dust, or mist. The faint of being unseen.

It could be passion. A former lover, a friend.
We would meet. A wine bar, dark corner table, a dim light swinging just off. The drinks sweat. We sip, we are the silent things.

SHE: Why did you get in touch after all these months?

ME: I wanted to give you something. I wanted to see if it had been as terrible as I have imagined. You look well.

32

SHE: I am. It's the reason I almost didn't come. I can't be thrown into your crazy again. You say wonderful things, but under it all you are just a monster. Just a creep. You need and you need, and there is no room. No breath. And I give. Because that is what I have learned to do. To follow, to value anyone else before me. I know I shouldn't, but it just happens and then I fall in. When I looked up I could not even remember how I had gotten so far away from me.

ME: It was not my intention.

SHE: I know, but that is not enough for me.

We drink. The silence is palpable, a breath on a neck, a hand tremble.

SHE: Is there something you want to tell me?

It would be then that I would pull out the short revolver, cock and aim for center mass. I would not be playing William Tell, I would be killing. I would watch the face I held dear collapse into questions, the eyes dim, the pain, a beautiful collapse. Chaos would ensue. The wine bar erupting into screams, and running. I would not make it to exit without firing several more times. Remembering to count the bullets.
five.
four.
three
two.

*************************The Power of Punishment is Hidden
to avoid recrimination, to appear just, gentle.

I am sitting in a street corner cafe with Michel, who is pontifi-
cating on his theory of discipline. He is a brain, wire thin, large
buldging eyes, thin mouth. He is a massive head, and he want
me to take a turn on the bottom.

Michel: I am always bottom, you should try it. It is in your
nature. I would be gentle, you would not even know at insert.

I consider this, as my cafe cools. He has a point. I am a bottom
by nature. I fear what this will mean. I fear that I will like it.
I am being erased. I know I am hetrosexual, but I have begged to
be freed from it all, not cease having to perform in-rigor male.

Michel: Punish art. I want to do a piece on punish arts.

Me: What would it look like?

Michel: The question should be what would it feel like. Say
that you have been judged guilty of say—theft. The panel may
decide from which era your mode of punishment will come
from. So, it could be that your hands would be lopped off, or
it could be just a jail sentence, which would be the far better
choice unless you are inside the prison, and then organizing,
or fighting. The solitary confinement would begin to pull away
at your ability to reason. I wanted to tell you of a dream, a
dream of wish-fulfillment that seems to be very in keeping
with the idea of writer, 4th wall and some such.

ME: Please, no more roundabout metaphors.

Michel: Surely you know the difference between a metaphor and a set piece?

ME: Yes, but to what end?

Michel: I thought we were in the business of killing the male centered novel?

ME: I'm not sure if it's wise to admit such things in public, let alone make it a part of the very novel you wish to kill.

Michel: Moving on, well for the purposes of bringing order to the elements of the HER in this, or any other novel we must discuss the HE that loves HER MOUF, and what the HE imagined it was for.

The image which is bandied about usually during adolescence has mainly to do with HER blowing HE. It was not until later that HE understood that in order to achieve the awesome power of the blowjob, especially when given in free will, without the usual tricks of coercion, and male-DOMO dick centric behaviors HE found himself becoming attuned to Cunnilingus, and kissing. Kissing became the opening portal.

At first HE kissed as a fish, all open MOUF. This evolved into sloppy wet spit, over chin, darting tongue like a lizard. No one corrected him until he found Sissy, who, in high school, was the fat girl foil to a gaggle of slim and blonde and coddled young women. Sissy was actually the one boys went to if there was the gumption of something past second base. She was a finisher, and understood her role, understood that sex was the ultimate equalizer. Everyone gets horny, and everyone must be pleased. So Sissy did not mind if the boys tried to thrust their crooked, mommy-made cocks at her face. She would take them in her chubby hand, and stroke them with the care one would show a small kitten, and then put them in her Mouf further and farther than a girl her age should know how to.

She understood a certain ball technique was the key to boy's erections, and if one could prolong the time before the suck then she could make these boys do whatever she wanted, if only because they were randy for a chance to finish thrusting her Mouf. By the time she was 20, she had shed most of her baby fat, and now could be considered Rubenesque, curvy, full figured in the Beat Culture sense. The white boys were the last to catch onto her curvy beauty.

Perhaps Her had come to your apartment before her shift once, for an early Christmas gift. You gave her a copy of Greer's The Female Eunuch. It took her seven months to get through the tome, but she was a determined sort, and struggled with the tenacity of a toothless man chewing a well done steak.

"There is no Thanatos, just Eros."

This interaction led to an arrangement, which is typically ideal unless you get emotional, and catch feelings. You connect her abilities to be the sign of actual passion for you. Her tolerates your need to make jokes, and your adolescent need for drugs; which coincidentally leaves you impotent. HER sucks and rubs your flaccid anyway, for hours, while you read, or pretend to write.

You: "I think I'm falling in love with you."

HER: "No, you just think you should. Its learned maleness."

You: "How can you say that I don't? You don't know how I feel."

HER: "Sure I do. You feel with your hands.

HE/You let the subject drop to avoid embarrassment.

Michel lights another cigarette, and pretends to twirl the smoke with his left index finger,

M: You want to know how she can suck your penis for hours while chastising you about learned maleness?

ME: Perhaps.

M: Its quite simple, one act does not cancel the other out. You have it in your head that a woman who performs fellatio would not be a feminist, let me take that back, would not have the nuance to hold your penis in her MOUF while discussing the patriarchal writer you are, and are created by. Which one of you is controlling this section, and who do I represent?
Too bad you cannot let yourself admit that you care for Sissy.

That Sissy is real to you, maybe she has different names, maybe she will save your life.

Suddenly, as if Marquez, Michel is gone, and I am laying in a field, the whole of me aching like a battlefield. in aftermath smolder, its on my face, even though I cannot see it, but my MOUF, cracked by wind, all of it, long ago. I try and gather moisture in the caked and destroyed hole of my MOUF, but spit has left a long while ago.

This long ago: consumes me in an urge to scream, and what I cannot control with my brain, I snuff out with my hands.

Had there been a CITI here? I remember it being destroyed, I remember it killing me. The day to day has left me. I walk along the old highway. No sound. Not even wind. I can hear myself slipping, the real and the lie. The time and its end. WE will let each other speak, for this is the story is all WE have. We will depend on each other to tell you it all. This is the story we have, caught in the MOUF of animals. The barely alive suffer too, and we kill. and we miss. But the missing is another story WE have caught in another book, another time.

HAND.

I.

She sat with just enough thigh, crossed legged at the knee. Her cig was always a dangle, and there was a wine stain always at play, her lips a thin eastern-euro. I was in love with her but not really. Mostly I was afraid, she liked no well enough because I listened to her even though most of it was the narrator and his tattered sentiment.

Sharon: So you know that Piano Bar where all those creepy Russian dudes hang?

I nodded yes.

Sharon: Well, I was there last week with that girl you see me with sometimes, Tracy. You know, the blonde with the chin acne.

Nod yes.

Sharon: We were drinking, and she had her ass up so our tab was still manageable and this tiny fat fucker plops down and offers us three hundred dollars if we will sit in his lap in the private room off the back of the bar. She immediately agrees, but he insists that we both do it, or no money. I'm fucking trying to get toasted on Fernet, and she trying to find her next mark so we agree even though we are nowhere near each other as far as our agendas. come on, you know how I do, so if I can get a free drink out of the deal then who am I to say no?

I light a cig.

Sharon: We go back, and he slides us three crisp hundred dollar bills. Three of the new face ones for each of us. Tracy sits down on his lap and he is smoking those fucking clove cigarillos like some fucking goth teen.

There are a few other men there, but its quiet. Some secret door opens and this fucking cocktail waitress, who happens to be the most meth-headed bitch I have ever seen comes over and takes our drink order, she slides up to one of the tables and drops a box of cigars on it. The men smack her on her flat ass, not hard, just little taps, and she gigles and walks off. A minute later she brings our drinks and the fat man struggles to pull a fifty out and tips her in the garter. Tracy is nestled in there pretty good, and I'm on my phone. He's got his fat fingers up the sides of her flairs, but his fingers are too short to reach her Boo parts, but you know the drill, he is making it with her, and she is oblivious, trying to catch the eye of one of the dudes sitting at the back table. They are watching the show, and every once in a while raise glasses toward us in a mocking toast. It's all very staid and boring yo.

Fat man is telling us about some house he has on the lake, and how he travels too much to use it and that she can use it when he's not there. She is giggly and stupid and I'm wondering why the fuck I hang with her stupid ass in the first place. We are about three rounds in when some other fucker with a really tight suit sits opposite of me, and begins to chat me up. He is slimmer than fat finger, but plain in the face, soft looking. Doughy even. With the flat eyes of a serial rapist on TV, never met any in real life, although there are some rapey looking dudes that hang around, like your friend Martin, or that bartender over at DE-lux, you know the one with the blond fon-du and all the tribal jewelry.

Me: That kid is harmless yo, what the fuck?

Sharon: How the fuck do you know? Shit what was I saying? Oh yeah, that dude is rapey as fuck.

She lights her sixth cig.

His nails are all lacquered up and he is sitting cross legged like some kind of 50's queen. Sipping on a virgin Daquiri. Money clip in his left hand like a lure. We begin chatting,

Him: Are you a member of the club?

Sharon: No. I'm here as a guest. You?

Him: Well not really, I own a portion of this place, just a small piece. Really it allows me to drink whenever I want, and occasionally host a private party in the lounge. My name is Kurt Utter, and yours?

Sharon: Sharon. Nice to meet you.

I extend my hand which he takes in his wet left.

HIM: I've been contemplating as we sit here what you are up to.

Sharon: How so?

HIM: Well for one, What do you do for a living?

Sharon: I work.

HIM: Come now, don't be coy.

Sharon: I'm not. I just tend to rather keep myself to myself, I don't know you dude. I am not sure if I want to.

HIM: Fair. Perhaps you would like another cocktail? Coincidentally, why is your friend allowing this man to grope her? Is that her business?

Sharon: You mean is she working? No, I think it's safe to say that she is fucking for free most times. Although she probably is not against gifts and favors.

HIM laughs.
You are quite a woman Sharon. Would you like me to show you something?

Sharon: Ummm… depends I guess. Fuck it, why not?

HIM stands up, and pulls out a small pistol. He does this casually and it seems that no cares to notice. Fat fingers sure doesn't, Tracy is too fucking dumb, and drunk too. So this suit stands up, and puts a bullet in both of their heads.

ME: WHAT?! Shut the fuck up, no way that happened. Come on, I'm listening you ain't gotta play games.

Sharon: Seriously he just strides around the table, and BAM, BAM two shots. Brains and blood everywhere, all over. Then he turns to me, and says you should probaly strip so we can dispose of the mess. I'm shaking like some crackhead, and he is all calm. I'm thinking he is gonna kill us all. The dudes at the back table haven't even looked up, so I ask,

"Why the fuck did you do that?"

And this creepy fucker just lights one of fat fingers cigarillos and says

"Because I can."

He picks up the house phone, and says into it - "Get me THE HAND."

Me: No way, you are so full of shit Shae.

My heart is racing, and I'm thinking I may just faint, but I keep it together and just look at her.

Sharon: So I strip, and we are all sitting in there naked as the day we were born. Thirty minutes go by and this tiny man with the most humongous hands come in, quietly locks the door and begins to tell us what to do, you know, so he can clean. By that point I think I'm going to die so I tell suit that I would like that drink now. Within two hours the scene is clean, and I spend the next three weeks with suit.

ME: So what you just hang out with this guy, and that's it? No more fat fingers, no more Tracy?

Sharon: Yep. That's the size of it.

ME: I still don't believe you.

Sharon: SO? That is what happened.

ME: Are you still seeing the suit? I mean, shit lady, is that where you been hiding? I haven't seen you in weeks.

Sharon: Yeah, well the guy has the biggest cock I have ever seen.

ME: WOW.

Sharon: Yep.

****

I am watching porn.

I have decided that my VHS tapes are the best option, the DVDs bore and I wish to go back to the time when I first started jerking my me. I dig out the machine, it is Feminine in design, the slot, a receiver of the taped patriarchy. It does not have a choice. If I push in the tape, it must receive it. It only plays back what it is given. Without tape it is just a blue screen, a flicker of static electricity changes it. Snaps it to rhythm, but it is blank, not full.

The first scene begins with canned Nu-Jazz, we catch the woman mid frame, beginning to shower, the camera pans up to her breasts which she elaborately soaps. More soap than it takes to clean, it is lube for you to begin. The social cue. You are the secret watching the private act. Down one leg, the middle soapy, two hands—one for her vagina (not shaven) one for her ass. The dramatic rinse, careful to not wet her hair. Done in the high 80's style of hairspray and large bangs.

The turning off of the water is the cue for you to begin catching a pulse, you stroke slow, trying to draw wood. She is now toweling off, the camera jump-cuts to the man, who is plain, same hair although parted down the middle. He is smallish in stature, and is wearing a blue stafford and a big red tie. He begins to take the tie off, and then it's back to the woman, who is now rolling up her stockings. One smooth leg, then the other. Her breasts are free, deep red buds as nipple. The man climbs the stairs, he enters the bedroom, she is now applying lipstick, he comes from behind sloppy kisses along her neck, his hand is already at hers. Loud paw.

You spill your load too early, and watch, the spent nut drying in hand.

There are a million reasons why I should not be telling you any of this, and I'm sure there are a few you will be able to guess. While we are not going to go with the postmodern you don't deserve it routine, it is partly true. The main reason I should keep this too myself has to do with THE HAND, who is quite capable of murder since he spends most of his nights cleaning them up. But I simply must tell you since this book is dealing with the concept of CITI(s) and that happens to be the only place someone like THE HAND could exist, even though the skills needed to "hand" are cultivated in strictly rural environs. Lawless barns, and country roads where sick little boys can practice their dismembering techniques, even to the point of alerting the local sheriff who will come around and have a stern but familial talking to the troubled young man because "Mrs. Fisher's dog and two of her goats have been missing, and Ole Fullers kid saw the young HAND was the last person around when the dog just up and vanished." The sheriff would add—"We all feel for you and your ma, cuz your poppa was a decent man, well respected, and we know y'all are still grieving but ya gotta stop killing the neighbor's pets. It's not Christian, well damn, it ain't too neighborly either. You want to do right by your daddy's memory, right boy?"

And young HAND would simply nod, and wring his HANDS just so. The sheriff would tip his hat, and walk off mutteriing about the sick little fucker, might have to put him down. And the resentment that the little talk created would fester, and smolder on for months after. The sheriff having forgotten the little talking to for having to do that with dozens of the other county boys. Would come home one night, and find that his dear sweet ole mama has been gutted like a Bass, and drained, he would later find out from the county coroner of all her blood.

She had been injected with a combination of bleach and milk in what the coroner could only describe as some type of big city metaphor. And even in his grief the sheriff would think about who could have done such a horrible thing, only to keep coming back to the one tiny ugly face young HAND. Sheriff being a pramatic civil servant would simply have to live with it, for his gut told him that the troubled young HAND was a nasty fucker and there was no telling how far he could go, what the limits of his depravity could be. He was the Devil's work.

So you can understand why me telling you what I may or may not be about to tell you could prove hazardous to breathing. It is not the murder that I've been seeking. Best believe I would rather eat out a baboons ass then tangle with HAND. Sharon had totally freaked me out with the Piano Bar story, but as a week, and then a month went by, everyone I ran into was telling me HAND stories.

HAND shows up at a little DIY punk house and gets rid of the sixty year old pederast organizer just because he cannot stand pedophiles; or, HAND shows up with two goons, orders a very dry martini while the goons whack the Korean owner for not paying protection. He wavers along this incredible moral judge situation, always swift in the vengeance quota when he is not jobbing for all the crooks in town.

I ran into a few kids I knew from shows at this hole in the wall I like to drink in. It was the middle of the day, and I needed a distraction for I was trying to stop smoking. They spied me before I saw them, and gestured for me to join their table. There was Sarah, who was a crackhead then, and had one of the biggest mouth-to-face ratios I have ever seen. She looked like the mother of a Sigourney Weaver nightmare. And then there was Harold who was round, but had a penchant for wearing his clothes several sizes too small, a human sausage link. He was also a fast talker, and a bit of a lesbian, but no one had the heart to tell that he was supposed to be one. The ringleader was this tall jaunty fucker named Matt who looked like Ichabod Crane, and Thurston Moore's baby. He had a deep voice that was damn near spot on for Robeson.
(Let's assume, reader, that you will be playing the role of Matt, AKA Ring.)

Ring: What you up to?

Me: Nothing much, which one of you mothafuckas gonna get me a well and soda?

Harold: I think that would be you.

Sarah: I got it, but you got to go get it, and bring me another Vodka cran.

Me: Will do.

Back with the drinks, which were done before I crossed my leg, making me wish I had taken a few shots to the face before sitting.

Harold: You got any pot?

Me: A pinch. We could cop some more.

Ring: Boring.

Sarah: I was thinking something a bit more adult.

Me: Oh, aren't we Miss Sophisticated?

Sarah: Bite me.

Me: I would rather you bit me.

Harold: You think we could score both, I'm assuming you want some Jackson, Sarah?

Sarah: No. Meth.

Ring: I'm the fuck out of here.

Sarah: You are such a fucking pussy dude. Let me borrow fifty bucks?

Ring: Ain't got no scratch for you crackhead. I'm not interested in any of this.

Me: OK Well I'm not doing any meth, but I would watch. I'm far more interested in getting drunk. Drunk is where I be at, but I can take you around to Fish your order up.

Sarah: Do we have to use Fish? What about Cushmere, or that dude Paul?

Me: Fish will have both. What's your problem with Fish?

Sarah: He's a creep. I fucking hate dealing with him. Can't keep his dirty fucking mitts to himself.

Harold: You can just wait in the car. Bob, can we use your place?

Me: Mi casa, su casa.

Sarah: Lets get another round. You got anything to drink at Weirdo Place Palace?

Me: A few loose beers, nothing heavy, but I was planning on stocking up. We can go around to the Arab store.

Sarah: But you can get to-go here.

Harold: Not everyone has a trust fund cuz they Daddy put it in their butt at twelve.

Sarah: Fuck you. I'm gonna invite Krissy if that's cool?

Me: Sure. Get me a double this time.

Harold: I got this, Sarah you want the same thing?

Sarah: Yeah, about as much as you want to be skinny.

Harold: You are such an asshole.

Sarah: Yeah, but you are all the assholes.

It takes about an hour to get to Fish's.
We order, he offers some samples, we take them. Lose track of time and hear Sarah honking the horn downstairs.

Fish: What the fuck is wrong with that cunt? I went out with her a few months you know? Bitch was smoking all my shit and wouldn't let me put a hand on her.

Me: Why should she?

Fish: Well that's usually the exchange. Free drugs, for some lush warm pussy.

Harold: Fucking creepy outlook, man.

Fish: What do you know about it, faggot?

Harold: NOW, NOW. You should keep your homophobia out of the customer experience.

Me: You should keep words out of every experience.

Fish: You two are assholes. Check this out. Traded it for an ounce.

Me: Is that a fucking sword?

Fish: No, its a saber. Pretty fuckin' tits, huh?

Harold: Why?

Fish: Come on, even yo soft ass wants a sword, shit who doesn't? This shit is medieval. Like I'm a knight.

Me: Dude, its a fucking saber, that shit cannot hurt a flea. Nothing knightly about it.

Fish: What the fuck do you know?

And then this silly fucka starts swinging the thing around, making lightsaber sounds and shit, doing these pansy jumps and thrusts. The thing almost takes the cat's eye, and he is winded from like a minute of dancing around.

Fish: Still working on my technique. Watching YouTube vids on it. By next year I will have my shit tight.

Sarah is all pout when we finally get back to the car.

Sarah: What the fuck? How long does it take to get yo' hands on some fucking drugs?

We spend the next 24 hours discussing what's better—Simpsons or Star Wars. Harold tries to give me a blowjob, but settled for giving Sarah one.

Citi falls in on itself, people dancing along the suffering, pretending to be advancing toward the middle, so the edges get harder to distinguish. Death is round the back doors, knocking, pretending to be Savior.

We wish for a coming grace, we hope that one of us will rise and make it better for all, take the weight that has fallen from our progress, from our striving. We cannot take the idea of not mattering, we will not allow for the simple fact that there is no help. Within our mushy meandering, there is meaning, and the meaning is not insightful. The meaning is the shell. There is a death that must come, we have built too much, so now nature revolts, the ghost of crimes long since forgotten rises. It is scary that this ghost is the mirror that we made.

****

Cush got tickets to go see Michael Eric Dyson speaks at State State University, and decided that I should accompany him. I hate lectures, but felt bad when I decided that I couldn't pay him for the Hash Candy. So I tagged along, wearing a crumpled blazer, and Chucks.

Cush picked me up rocking a Dashiki.

Me: The fuck you got on?

Cush: No, not gonna fall for it. You always get all judgy when you are uncomfortable. Here, smoke this, and shut the fuck up.

Me: Will do.

We ride in silence. Cush doesn't like to drive on the highway so we take the city streets from the deep west end, to downtown where State State is.

Cush: You know anything about Dyson?

Me: Heard him on TV talking about Marvin Gaye once. Total preacher blowhard.

Cush: You are such a boring-ass hater. He has a lot to say about urban culture, and commercialism. His new book is about authenticity in Black America.

Me: There is no such thing as authenticity. We are all actors and fakers and cowards. Suicide should be mandatory.

Cush: How's the joint?

Me: WOW. You really are excited. You gonna just let that go?

Cush: I'm not engaging you. Fucking sick-hearted fucker, but I do love you.

Me: Is that the best you can do?

Cush: Fuck you. I'm not writing any of this.

Me: So we are just tropes, no free will, eh?

Cush: We are set pieces in the loose fragment of a philosophical novel. Besides, fuck is a great word. But boring to read, awesome to say, miserable to read.

There is a concept that has become widely accepted as Gospel—let me be clear—it is a mainstream truism, but it pervades generationally, and leaves a very two-dimensional concept of blackness. Authenticity is the topic of First World privilege. Let's be clear, that within our world community, no one is much concerned with a superficial racial, ethnic authenticity. Divisions—of real and of death consequences is occurring all over the globe. These divisions, along tribal, ethnic and religious lines are ancient. There is no denying our human need to group and name. To create difference when biologically there is little evidence of any. The heart, the brain, the liver, the lungs—operate as if there is only one kind of person, sentient. Walking upright with language centers, reasoning, and a natural predilection toward domo-violence.

Human. We are human. The dividing lines are man-made, and they always have been, always will be.

So we have gotten the generalities out of the way, let's see if we can answer this unspoken, misunderstood concept of authenticity. Let's assume that we are aware that the New World was built upon a system of human bondage, racial genocide, land seizure, and indentured European servitude. Let's assume that we are all aware that over 11 Million Africans were brought to the new world under the extreme and often lethal practice of the slave trade. Over the course of two centuries, this practice, the very idea of where these Africans originated from has fallen away, along with their native languages, musics, and cultures. We must understand the concept of a continent. A continent is not just one country, it's typically a grouping of countries, or lands, and each grouping, or land or country, has its own set of traditions, music, culture and leadership structures. Remember that we have already established that human beings are naturally predisposed to grouping and naming. The identification of the Other is as natural to us as breath. It is also the genius, and the failure of humanity.

How can one action be so polarizing?

The critical response is important, but let's continue. So with the falling away of the concept of where we are from, we begin to build traditions here in the New World. Anthropological studies can connect these new traditions, this new African-ness, with an unremembered past, the hints are what some social scientists call Genetic Memory. This Genetic Memory becomes even more powerful when coupled with trauma. Trauma is the ultimate sealer, it fuses experience to our DNA in ways even our most brilliant thinkers cannot understand.

Let's skip to the Civil War, well, we can take up the thread a year into the reunification of North and South. Slavery has been abolished, leaving a huge gap in the economic might of Southern Industry simply because new work must be paid.

Southern culture has not really changed, there are still some who believe that their new citizens—former slaves—still should be enslaved. The control methods of African inferiority still a prevailing logic, even though federally there is no concept of slavery. Words like Negro, Nigger, Coon are still widely used. North or South. The connection to this racial divide is never connected to a class question in most instances. Poor whites are now worried that they will have to compete with freed slaves for physical labor. With the tripling of the unskilled workforce, the ground was set for a clash.

The existence of a new American-African culture is in full swings and what was formerly considered field songs combines with Old World cultural work songs and bar sing-alongs to create a new American music—country songs (white), blues and gospels songs (black), even though the music borrows from each other, and is nearly unrecognizable as far as its musical parts in our post modernity.

These American songs became the backbone of the working class, and the performing of them creates a new industry in the next century. By the early 1900s the practice of these work songs, these American hymns, is firmly entrenched. So much so, this American music becomes the chief cultural export of the US to the outside world, and sets us on a journey of being a nation of dynamic cultural creators.

Strides are made, black men are given, or rather fight for the right to vote and the country surges into the industrial age full of promise, ingenuity, and opportunity, both financially, and culturally. Those words still—NIGGER. Today, this word has come alive, and is still the invention of a more politically correct version NIGGA, BLACK, COLORED. Whichever one suits the time and manner. Racial violence still raises its ugly KKK Head. It is just as potent now, if not more so, than during our country's slave beginnings. This is not to say that all people of African descent have not been able to take advantage of the free market design of our country. They have, they do. And what does all of this mean when we are discussing the concept of authenticity?

It Happens in slow motion. A man walks up the aisle of the auditorium, and when he passes our row I barely notice. Dyson is in full preacher throat, hands extended, and from behind Pop, Pop and then red shirt. Again Pop, Pop, barely audible over the screams and pushing.

Pop, Pop.

It takes me thirty minutes to find Cush, huddled up along the sides of a far row of seats. His dashiki fully torn, showing his kidney scar like a MOUF.

**************************HEARD on the street that HAND is looking for me. Don't know exactly why; probably doesn't even matter why. If he finds me, he will kill me. The thought of being murdered is a bit off-putting. It is nowhere near as euphoric an exercise as planning to kill. And it's not the frank and innocent giving up of suicide. In all of this, I find myself serene in the knowledge that perhaps any day, hour, minute could be my last.

For the purpose of books has always been some sort of 'moral'-ness, the authority of the holy, as if the sitting on one's ass and lying can be anymore than what it truly is. It is not the solitary act the romantic commerical depicts, it is symbiosis of reader and writer. Without either, the literature cannot happen. The strange thing is, the exchange of currency is never the true value of the transaction. It is the cash I seek. I have had enough time.
"TIME IS MY ENEMY, SAILING A PAPER SHIP"
Sir Gil Scott once said. And again the HAND is looking for me. If I try and find out why, it could make matters worse. If I don't, the book is dead, our relationship ceases, and then I will be alone, clutching the half-formed mass in my left paw, claiming to be Yogi Bear, or worse some sort of nigger wrestler who has read Proust.

If I hide, then what? So I decide to do my normal routine, but I keep myself on swivel, hoping he won't sneak up and gut me. It would be a shame for folks to see me dead in the street, my guts spilling on the gentrified pavement. They would then see how much Wendy's I can eat. Drugs are out, and Cush is in North Carolina visiting his sister to recover from us witnessing that replay of the Malcolm Assassination. Dyson's face is plastered all over the news, speeches are being made, the pundits are awoke!

Obama says he will not rest until the assassins are bought to justice, whomever killed Dyson picked the wrong guy. He was not a leader, he was a talking head, and second-tier thinker. The old Cointelpro modes do not work without messiahs. This is an age without angels.

I'm sitting in Lou's Place in Southside when HAND walks in. He is carrying a metal attache' case, and has his goons with him. He sits down after carefully folding his overcoat, and sneers in that weak tremble he calls a voice:

"Bobby. Been looking for you. Do you know who I am?"

Me: Everyone knows who you are.
                    I down my drink, finger up another.

HAND: Are you curious as to why I am looking for you?
                    I get my drink and shake my head: NO.

HAND: Well you should be a bit interested given my profession.

Me: No. Not really, since I'm just a drunk who pecks at stories. I don't move in your world Mr., never will, wouldn't want to.
I surprise myself with the courage in my voice, and then panic when it dawns on me I'm just drunk.

HAND: You got a funny manner Bobby. I have to admit, you got some balls on you. Maybe you are a bit too foolish, maybe you are just playing tough guy for the sake of the readers. Who knows? But this ain't no choose-your-own-adventure story you fat fuck, this ain't no gangsta novella either, this is real life. What I have in this case is my papers. I want you to do me a favor, and edit my story down for the purposes of a memoir. I'm going to retire, and I need some seed money. I'm gonna sell my story for State's evidence and get me a nice clean life.
    He smiles invisibly. I tremble over my drink. I'm finding that

swallowing is becoming difficult.

Me: Not really my gig. I make stuff up, not a journalist, you got to find someone else. Besides if the evil fuckers that employ your scary ass find out I helped you, out on the morgue slab I go.

HAND: You are going to be paid handsomely. You need the money. You think this novel is gonna make you big? You are always gonna be a minor league bum. This could launch you in ways your stupid brain never could. Inside the case are twenty stacks. I will be around to collect in ten days. Do not have me come looking for you. Morris here is gonna drive you, and keep you on task. No drugs. No bullshit. Completed manuscript in ten days, our patience and time are spent. You will not catch a break.

Me: Understood. Morris, right? No drugs. By the way, why me?

HAND: My daughter Sissy, as you know her, Cynthia to her mother, and Cindy to me says that you two have an understanding, and that you have been a gentleman and a fool for much of it.
Me: She is a good…

HAND: Watch it.

THE INSOLENCE which desecrated my face was the fact that I was two days late with HAND's manuscript, which caused him to be picked up by the Feds, and me to be MOUF cut.

The two cops, Flatends and Jobson have been trying to bust me for months now, they have it in their dull skulls that it will make their careers and that detective-grade shields will be issued. Parades are not given to cops who bust drunk and stupid writers. CITIS is full of them, each one with his own conceits, and marginal talents, each one with a loyal and small army of fans. The really good ones are hated by their mothers, and the best are usually women.

Which is why many male writers tend to draw them as set pieces for a man's dilemma. Politics aside I must admit to you that I was born a woman, but my parents thinking my clit was too large, had my sex changed. This would be embarassing if the doctors had not been able to form a very handsome and quite impressive penis no matter how flaccid it now is for drug abuse, fear, and self-loathing.

They pick me up four days before I am supposed to meet HAND and turn in the manuscript.

(The following is a transcript of the arrest, detention and abuse at the hands of these two nitwits):

Jobson: Where ya headed, Bobby?

Me: Minding my own business officer, but if you must know I am off for supplies.

Flatends: Don't be so cute nigga, you ain't Cosby. Come over here.

Me: Is there a problem? I really have to get going. I'm on deadline.

Flatends: We know you do, Bob. We been onto you for months.
                                                    I laugh and light a cig.

Me: Please spare me the hardboiled shit, you fuck, I have neither the time, nor am I required to talk to you.
        Jobson grabs me up, I let him fearing that he will shoot me.

Jobson: All you got is time you fucking lowlife. We've been watching you for months, we know when you go shit mothafucka.
                                        I stay quiet as they pat me down.

Jobson: Why you got so much walk around cash on you? Gerry, you see this? Fucker's got like a grand on him.

Flatends: Why so much cash, you going to pay off your dealers? Put your hands on the hood.
        I do as they say, and they pat me down for the third time.

                                                                    Cuff me.

Me: What the…

                                                    Then tazed to my side.

I wake up in a holding cell smelling like I shat myself.

HOUR TEN is when I realize that I did shit myself. I'm in a holding cell with three teenaged drug mules, a half dozen drunk, but still able-bodied middle-aged white men, and one killer who resembles what Hollywood thinks Tonto looks like. Of course Tonto is the talkative one. Homicide makes you chatty.

Tonto: I snapped his fucking neck. I was tired of him drinking my beer, and pretending that he didn't. The fucker deserved it. Told him over and over don't touch my beer. You can drink my wine, smoke my bud, but if you drink my beer I am going to kill you.

Me: OK. I will bite. Who did you kill?

Tonto: My son. That fucker been drinking my beer.

Me: You killed your own son? Shit man, you should be locked up.
                                                    I start to panic,
GUARDS, Guards get me out of this cell.

                              The chubby sarge comes over,

Sarge: SHUT THE FUCK UP. You want me to place you on a Psych Hold?

Tonto: You just don't understand. I didn't want to do it, he made me.

Me: How old was he? Should we say a few words in his memory?

Drug Mule Big Lip: Man, ya can stop that shit my dude. You both ain't ready for hard time.

Tonto: WHAT DID YOU SAY?
Drug Mule Big Lip: I said shut the fuck up you fucking Indian.

Tonto: I thought that's what you said.

Me: Now, look we don't need any violence. We got enough trouble. Fellas, let's be pals.

Drug Mule Big Lip: You just shut the fuck up, you Uncle Tom-ass nigga.

Me: No need to racialize the situation. Didn't you fucking assholes just hear what the man said? Our fine Native American friend here just said he killed his own son for drinking his beer. BEER.
Just when Drug Mule Big Lip was about to say something Tonto had his massive HANDS around the kid's neck, lifting him like he was a small child, and then awful sound of a neck breaking.

Drug Mule Skinny Neck: Damn yo' he killed 'em just like that, he just fucking killed him!
The cell door opens and in come a dozen officers with billy clubs and tazers at the ready.

Me: WAIT, I didn't…
BAM. Tazed for the second time in twenty-four hours.

[I didn't get released for another seventy-two hours due to lack of evidence.] Flatends and Jobson follow me to the bus stop, and actually ride with me to my place. I am met by the HAND's goons who take me upstairs as the shitty cops watch, laughing and snapping pictures with their phones.

WE are upstairs. Goon One is a bit like Lurch, but with the kind of dead eyes only a dead mother could love.

Goon Two, Morris, is straight out of Micky Spillane, College Joe-type Jaw. Seems to think he is Brad Pitt, when he is really a middle-aged Mel Gibson.

Mel is the talker.

Morris: Where is HAND's manuscript you dip shit?

Me: Why do you people insist on using diminutives for me? I'm 6 foot and weigh 270 pounds.

Morris: Yeah, but you are light-weight just like the rest of you arty fucks.

Me: Has anyone ever told you that you look like Mel Gibson?

Morris: Cut the shit. Are you finished?

Me: Can I have a cig?

Lurch hands me one, and grunts twice, which is monster for "Cut the shit."

Me: (after two puffs) I ran into a bit of trouble and need just three more days. You see…

Lurch backhands me, and my whole left side goes numb.

Mel: You got a lot of nerve, look they picked HAND up because you were late with his manuscript.

Me: Well that makes no sense.

Mel: No shit, fucktard. You are the one writing this stupid shit. Got me looking like Mel Gibson, you bastard.

Me: Wow. A character who takes it personally.

Mel: We got to get this thing buttoned up, and move on to the next scene. How bad do you want us to fuck up your face for "Plot's" sake?

Me: Just a tad. Wait? I didn't want you to say that.

Mel: Well, sometimes characters get a mind of their own, you douche.

Me: WAIT… If I'm writing, but I am also a character, who really is the writer?

****

Turns out Lurch is an excellent cook, we ate rather well while I turned around THE HAND manuscript. For goons they were quite pleasant, and after a day I could see the finish. This surprised me because I was working with a couple of busted fingers, a swollen eye, a destroyed MOUF—as my punishment for missing the initial deadline.

My lips were fatter than engorged vulvas, and far less attractive, but what can you do? I had street cred if I could survive, for I had defied THE HAND and was not gutted with a kitchen knife. As I went through HAND's journals and papers I was struck by how well he wrote, and the quality of detail he could generate. It was unclear if he wrote immediately after a job, or would let memories collect until he had a day's worth of entries to work on. Since none of his actual testimony will be sealed I thought I would treat you to some highlights.

On Killing Women

It's never as much fun to kill a woman. They tend to have not really done anything other than resist possession, which would typically drive their powerful male pursuers crazy. Big time criminals tend to the invention of them being exceptional citizens.

Really, they are just hoods with suits, and any sophistication that they have come into is usually the product of the illegal gains, and the very women they want dead. Passion is the delusion drug, and if a woman resists this Mook's efforts to keep her for himself, and the woman decide that his evil, coupled with a non-functioning cock, is not worth the tremendous misogyny at the base of his want to keep her. Or—and this happens more than you think—if her heart gets caught by one of his underlings it is she who will be punished, even though she was pursued by the young worker. Men protect men, and women are taught to protect them as well. I would always try and make it painless when I was hired. A job is a job; you must always finish the job.

ON FAVORITE JOBS

One of my most enjoyable jobs was to put fear into some fool quarterback for the CITI team. The dude is still alive, and I, like so many, are rather fond of him, so I will leave his name out of it. It all started with me showing up to his big ole house, and cutting the power. This guy was so beloved by the community that he had no security; stupid hick didn't even lock his door.

I got in there, tied him to a chair. Using my favorite knife from my father, I cut tiny holes in his stomach, maybe a quarter of an inch thick in diameter. You can tell a lot from a cut, how the person reacts can show you just how evil they are, or how dumb. It's always different, you never can predict until the cuts. I carved "CHOKE ARTIST" into the golden boy's stomach, you can imagine this happens to be the worst thing you can call a professional athlete.

The fucker just cried, and I began visit him regularly to make sure he wasn't gambling. You see, I was hired by the owner of the team to take care of problems like this. I was to keep him straight, but not straight enough that the team would succeed. The owner was a creep, and a crook. He only wanted the team to be good enough that he could pressure the city for a new stadium. He had his fucking hands in everything. Whores and dope, price-fixing and shell games, always siphoning off the earning sheets. I would have loved to kill him. Instead, he kills his wife and step-daughter and I get the call to clean it up. It was one of the few times in all these years that I almost let a guy get pinched. The fuckers he was tied to would have sent someone to off me, but it might have been worth it.

I was able to get some background information on HAND, about his early life which validated my thoughts about him. He did grow up on a farm in Burton, Ohio and his father went to Korea when HAND was only a toddler, so he didn't know him. He grew up in a town where everyone, well-meaning or not, would comment about his father, how much he looked like him. This would enrage young HAND and he took to committing acts of violence. First, on birds and insects, then his neighbor's pets, and finally, classmates.

He left home after 17 and moved to Chicago where he worked as a cub reporter for The Reader and spent his days angling to get assigned to the city beat. For four years he apprenticed until he had enough connections and blackmail leverage to move up. The bit of blackmail that sealed the deal was when he caught the Metro editor in a compromising position with two very young Negro boys. Although what he saw was to form his life long disgust with rapists and pedophiles, he was crafty enough to use the information to his advantage.

No one ever questions how the ambitious creep found himself in hotel in the first place, but from his journal I was to ascertain that he was nursing a small habit. Mostly a few "grains" of heroin a month; at its worst, speedballs, and two "grain" a day habit.

He was a good reporter, and would have been a genius if not for his dark secret. He was a bloodletter, and he craved it; this did nothing for him as a junkie. It was that blood call that finally got him to kick. His career was going at a good clip, and he met a young teacher that he was falling for. Let's call her Laura. She loved HAND, and he melted into the possibility of starting a life with her. His bloodlust faded in his pursuit of a regular life. This passage was taken from one of his journals:

She had eyes that seemed to taste you rather than see you. Raven hair which always moused over her ear and fell into soft focus against the curve of her mouth. The first time I saw her she was sitting in this cozy spot on the lake, just watching. Just taking it in. Calm, above the fray, she was wondrous, and I followed her that day, and watched her move in the world with child-like wonder. I was to find out later that she knew I was following her, had spied me instantly. Some detective I was then. Sloppy. Unformed. When I finally had the courage to speak, she was the one who suggested we attend a movie. The formalities were set in motion. Laura suggested that we meet at the movie house, and buy tickets, and then if we bought the same movie ticket, we would spend the night, if we didn't it was not meant to be. As fate would have it, she chose The French Connection and so did I. We watched it, and got a late snack at the 24hr diner around the corner from her walk-up.

We spent the night. And after we were never apart for six years. She led me through it all. She was a tiger, she knew how she wanted to live, I had never given any of it much thought. We were happy, and then it was over.

HAND never goes through what occurred, but its safe to assume that she is no longer breathing, and that his daughter is with another woman, for Sissy does not resemble him, or the memory of Laura. Whatever did occur surely pushed him into the business of the HAND, and for the next thirty-five years he lived the spartan life. The record of clean-ups, murders and other death crimes that he either witnessed, or directly participated in, is impressive; a long winding history, the blood, the pulse of a corrupt machine. CITI was dying, and HAND was a nick of the mainline vein.

I was to see him one final time after finishing. Lurch, Mel, and I were sitting in a navy blue Lincoln Town Car toward the back of a No Parking Zone of the Justice Center and we saw him. Head down, the slow-step always. Federal Agents surrounding him in the protection his skill set always provided without assistance. He gracefully enters the unmarked SUV, and disappeared as HANDS never do.

COCK.

THERE is no such thing as security. The very thought of it turns patriotism into full-on zealotry; turns men into protectors, when, at most, they can only hope to protect themselves. For two hundred years, men have withered under the role. Of course there have been exceptions, and there have been extremes, where men sneak along alleys, their zippers sounding off like lions, their wives and children asleep in suburban slumber. They are hunting for the boy, hunting for the moment where their played-up role of protector can fall away in the mouths of each other. The sucking catalyst to continue the charade. Of course there are some who want nothing of that mask, and are free to love and fuck and suck as they please, but this is not of this. (THAT?)

I'm inching toward knowing a cock. I have spied him. In his jeans and daddy chin, the stiff posture of an underwear model. The ass of a boy. He downs beer. He is a large thing, and a shiny ring to pluck. I know he would not want me. He wishes no one to know that he secretly hides in the gutters, the shame of a million sins cum-stained to his lips.

(melodrama!)

I watch him at the bar, he never approaches the pussy in the room, lots of it mesmerized, like I am by his hands, by the maleness that exudes off his skin like the sheen of a jogging lather. We will call him Frank for the sake of literary history, and since it makes a neat but corny metaphor.

I watch the barkeep pour me another, and another. The shots

adding to my courage better than any drug should. I am half-hearted and beaten down by the prospect of this ending, the glory of the word, and then another. The end of this, and us together. You have been a good reader so far, Dearheart.

I nerve up and join the edge of the bar where Frank is holding court. I've been having dreams, the kind where your childhood comes out and attacks what you know of yourself, what you think you are. The mirror reflects nothing, for you are never willing to look long enough. The buried, somewhere, gut deep, the question: Am I really just a gay man, shamed into hetro-normal?

I have failed to love every woman I have known, the intimate designs of a liar. I want to know. I am outside of myself now, wanting my 'me' to melt into his hands like so many could, the will of a dozen Baldwins, in a night where only Othello[s] are rewarded. Tug at the end. Ass up. Alive and full.

THERE are four bores huddled around Frank, each trying to be Beta, like dogs at the pound. The wagging is in perfect concert with his conceit.

Bore 5 is a red-nosed little punk, with a mousy demeanor, he is probably still a virgin.

Then, there is 4, who is one those Oxford Negroes with the perfect Magic Shave and Clarence Thomas-level creepy. He comes off quite rapey, and proud of it. In ways, he is not proud of his skin. 3 is classic Tommy Hilfiger. He is a catch too, and knows it. Tight blond curls, and spray ocean eyes that seem as empty as his wallet. 2 is the token Asian, with the perfect wire rimmed specs and little body. His only body detail worth noting is the shelf level ass on the kid, if there was a natural bottom, he is it. Lets add a bit of intrigue: HE'S PAYING FOR EVERYTHING!!!

Frank is a prettier version of Vincent Gallo. The Gallo his mother hoped would show up before she died of lung cancer and a broken heart from her son's mediocrity. They don't seem to be saying anything of note, just doing as dudes do, with the cleverness of five year-olds at the circus. Women seem to fall into the learned behavior of accepting the marching, for it's a slave auction, just as dangerously inhuman, just as insidious.

Bore 2: Look at that one, she is checking you, Frank.

Bore 5: For sure, man she got a nice rack, and her friend can get it too.

Frank: Naw, she an ouchy.

Bore 3: What the fuck that mean?

Frank: When you give her that dick, she be saying 'ouch, ouch, ouch and ouch!'

They all laugh at this as if well-endowed means 4 ½ inches of half-hard and ugly circumcised cock.

Frank: Now that one in the red. She is fine for sure.

They all look. Frank looks away, and our eyes meet. I try to bore into him, but he is oblivious in his role and ignores it.

Bore 2: I should go over there and make it happen.

Bore 4: There is no way you could. You suck man, got the game of an old man.

A few of them laugh, but it lasts two beats.

Frank: Like you could do better.

Bore 4: I can have that girl creaming her panties right now.

Bore 3: Do it then Romeo.

Bore 4: Fuck you man, she's not really my type.

That sends them all into hysterics.

Bore 2: Frank, fucking get her over here man, and we can see what's what.

Frank: Naw man, she cool, but you got to do your own seducing. Get yo' game up.

> I am numb from the attempted Wigger speech,
> but let it go and order another drink.

I am thinking of drugs, but there are none. Just the meandering of the scared and the lifeless. Looking for connection, for a love promised by a father that hated you as a child anyway.

I catch back into Frank's denizens.

Frank: We should blow this place, ain't no action here. This shit is beyond boring.

Bore 4: Shit man, you could make it happen. I don't know why you always play so above the fray.

"What the fuck you even talking about?"

> Out of nowhere, a tight little redhead has
> appeared, biker jacket cocked over her
> shoulder, questioning eyes a bit blurred from
> drink.

Frank: Who the fuck are you?

"My name is Frannie, and I've been sitting at the bar watching you fags discuss women's bodies so I figured I would come over and offer some critique. Besides, what are you going to do about it? You so in the closet you might as well be an easter suit."

Frank: You small like a Hobbit. How I know you ain't packing a sword instead of a clit?

Bore 5: Frannie right? You wanna drink?

Frannie: Nope. Not from you, I got my own wad, you fucking douche.

Bore 5 - Hostile.
>   Frannie take center court, with Frank pouting
>   like a child with a dropped ice cream cone. His
>   father all angry cuz it dropped all over the back
>   of the mini van.

Frank gets brave and tries to wrest control of his minions. "You come here a lot? You seem to know the place."

Frannie: Yeah, my brother owns it. So who's fucking who?

Bore 2: Fuck that noise.

Bore 5: Damn right.

Frannie: You know what? I am gonna prove that you guys are gay.
>   She winks at Frank, and goes over to a group
>   of women, and begins to chat them up. After
>   awhile she comes back, women in tow.
Frannie: Fellas, this is Shelly, Joan, Renee, Amy and... Lee.
>   Frannie is all smiles.
Frannie: I got the first round. Tequila shots here we come!

Renee: Um... I pass, get me something on tap.

Frannie: Fuck that noise chick! Shots! Come on Frank, help me carry em back.

I watch them pair up awkwardly as Frank follows Frannie to the bar. They seem to be in a deep discussion with each other by the time they round the corner. I chuckle wondering if they are discussing Shakespeare, or just talking drugs. I decide that it's neither. No longer here, mainly because I am black-out drunk. I pay. Leave.

Wandering the streets like an alley cat that just got Nip. The wonder of the street light, a glow, wet along the slick. My mind aflutter on a lake wind. My shirt tails out, and the money is looking.

I told you of a dream, I cannot say that it's recurring, it changes, shifts in detail. This is the fifth night in a row. It always starts with a small blue frame house. There is a stumped stone fence complete with a wide and cracking bench surrounded by day lilies. Wildflowers.

Then.
A hallway. There is a woman, small in stature. She is important to me, but I do not know why. Her features fade from sharp edges to blank, the shifting, an electric scoreboard of face. Eyes. Blue to green to gray to brown eyes. MOUF, full and thin.

She is holding a child, but the child is the color of a blood orange. No sound until a flash, and then two awe shuck booms. The flash disappears, everything is black. I try to rush to them, cover them, but I cannot get there. The hallway seems to be growing under my feet. I am running, running. Then blown back.

Awake in a field.

The air does not move.

I am outside, and the leaves do not choir. The air is thick fog. I am bleeding from my head, my face.

I'm tired. So tired.

I awake to a knock on the door. Two stiff thumps. I let my eyes adjust and say:
"Just a minute."

When I open the door there is a blast, what looks like fire and then the heat. I come to in the clinical light of white, I open my eyes, but they are covered in medical gauze. I can make out voices, but cannot really hear what they are saying. I move my fingers along the bed, and try to lift myself.

The pain takes breath, then firm hands.
"You've been shot. You really ought not move. Just rest, the doctor will be in to discuss your injuries, but you had extensive surgery, and almost died on the table."

A certain type of man imagines women spend all their time flaunting themselves to inflame his senses.
—Virginia Woolf

I awaken to a sponging off, the gauze is gone, and the nurse looks a bit like Sargent Slaughter, or some Old-school wrestler. The water is too cool, I am wiggling.

Nurse Slaughter: Stay still, I must wash you. Starting to smell like a corpse. How'd you feel? Oh, I got to empty yu'r poo bag. How's yu'r pain?

Me: I need a phone. Please, I need to make a call, no one knows I am here.

Nurse Slaughter: Of course they do. Your wife has been here everyday. Yu'r having a hard recovery, but yu'r on the mend.

Me: I am not married.

Nurse Slaughter: That's just the drugs talking, of course yu'r married. and she's a real fox too. How the hell did someone like y'ur end up with a wife like that? Must be… well I would marry yu'r wife in a second.

Me: Can I get up?

Nurse Slaughter: NO. Not yet. YU'R STITCHES! They will be

removed in a few days, and then staples for your release. Lie still I got to wash yu'r bum.

I stay silent, nothing is more humiliating than someone washing your ass, but I'm too weak to protest, too dead to even care. Then the Morphine hits, the warm trickles down through the throbbing, a blankety for a newly minted eunuch.

Someone is holding my hand. Their fingers caressing along the tubes, rubbing at my fore-knuckle.

Her: Bobby, thank God you are alright. You had me worried.

I focus on her face, flipping through the pages of faces I've known.

Her: Do you need anything, you were moaning in your sleep.

Me: No.

Her: We will get through this. It's gonna be alright, I'm so glad you are still alive.

Me: I do want some water.

Her: Here you go, there. You want more? Slow, there you go.

Me: Where's Cushmere?

Her: He went to clean up your apartment. You get to come home today.

Me: How long have I been like this?

Her: You have been here 20 days, give or take. Do you need anything?

Me: No. Will you be staying?

Her: Bobby, I'm not here. I am from before. I am from your life before. Before, before.
You just needed me, and knew I should come.

Me: But… the nurse said…

Her: The nurse was me. This is all me.

Me: What do you mean? Am I hurt? Am I dead?

Her: Shhh… relax. Don't worry, I have taken care of everything. You said once that you would do anything to not be a man.

She was quiet, and searched my face.

Her: You no longer are, I fixed everything for you. You don't have to worry.

Me: What... do you mean? I wasn't... I... what did you do?

Her: I removed the instrument of your misery, the reason you have never had a good life. You do understand, don't be dense. Your cock, your penis was holding you back, keeping you in a patriarchal trap, keeping you in sin. But more than that, you hurt people. You take. Now you cannot do that anymore. You will be neither male, nor female. This is what you always wanted.

Me: What did you do? ... you can't be serious. I was just ...
                    The morphine is speaking, the warm inside the
                    throb.

Her: I had to. Of course I had to stop you. You begged me to save you, begged me. You have always lived within the confines of your sex. You thought yourself to have privilege. To be special. You are not special, you are not unique. I have saved you from this. I need you to sleep now. Just SLEEP.

Me: Wait! I have questions. I want to know who you are. What did I ever do to you?

Her: I am a cunt. I am everyone you ever lied to, every woman you ever dismissed, cheated on. Hurt. I am the hurt. Do you understand?

Me: But why ME? ALL OF THEM, ALL OF THEM ARE ASS-HOLES. WHY? Why are you punishing me?

Breath left me. I heaved for it. Reached for it. The gasp came.

Her: You asked for it.

There is a field, the clearing. I am alone. The CITI, a rubble of dust, invisible. No sound. It takes me some time to realize I am crying.

WE

are

the fragmenting.

Things.

Suppose there is a line, a line which you cannot cross, but your love, your self-preservation, butts up against it, daring you to leap.

Daring you to shed the cowardice you have clung to. The mess you allow to fester as you fear—the awesome testament, the first emotion, the one that bridges to the others, a telling mother. Fucking you.

The hours of you choked by denial. The buried deep of your primal voice, and what she wishes you would say. I've come wishing for more than a gone. The me of Me. But still a gone, that piece, the main thrust of my thinking.

The feeding of it, the lust images building behind the eye, behind what I knew of love, of faith, and the faithful cows in pasture, dying the slow, borrowed death.

Yes, the piece of me that I held in my meaty fist against the sink, a quick rub to a memory, the breasts heave subjective. Oh how I remember her MOUF on mine. On her. The MOUF. I run down the times. I jerk it in public stalls during my freshman year of college. I yank with a backhand Kung-Fu grip against the back wall of a punk club after she hands me her panties, and husky whispers my name as I fingerbang the velvet.

The all of me hoping for a blow. The piece of Me me. Risking a life with AIDS for a corner blowjob from someone's mother, who's too rock-gone to charge a living wage. Her day is seconds, to minutes and back. The again of it, the tangible need makes her more human than you could ever be.

I stop her mid way through, and finish myself with a hand on a decaying tit, the stretch marks of abandoned children—who will sing for her. My nut against the concrete. Those poor and cowardly nuts acts as the glue of the CITI. Politicians, Police, Pastors, all fisting the privileged member. The piece of me gone now.

I think about my wishing it to be gone, for it all to be erased, like I was never born a man.

****

Awhile ago I found a stash of photographs. They were of her, a her I cannot remember. I thought of myself as just, an ally. When really I was a mess of Fathers, the scared clutching of an inheritance that by rite of skin would never be mine.

YES. I am the failing things. Yes, I am the fall. Sure, there were times when I wished it away, where I tuck, The Wild Bill in the mirror, my house coat open. The imagined wind of an uncolored swept hair or some type of slim artifice of belonging.

And she we would say "I just want you."

And I would answer just love me as if had nothing left to give. Oh, to give, a prayer to the falling, all my men are mist, and the erection is tied to my asshole, and its health. So now it is gone.

I am home now. Cushmere has cleaned the apartment, and it feels as if I have died. My things filed in the nooks of a three floor walk-up. I open the windows to let in the CITI. You hear the cars, their horns in the cat-call of impatience, the occasional siren, the yelling—the whispers of street deals, the soup of poverty. The day-to-day of the eventual. The Lords lord over us, shiny towers girded with opulence. All of us wishing for a deep nut, like we deserve Her curve, and honey supple. The caress of hoping.

I look out of the window, the chain-smoke creating a painting of a weak mind. I let the phone ring, I let the sound wash out. It's my first day without the piece, the piece that held me male. Am I a man without the Me member? The liberal would say of course, but they do not control definitions. Those are made deep in the Money Tower. After 300 years and change, my line is ending.

Me without a nut to give, a fuck to master. I will take this story and write a line of blood, on the lead, blood, mighty forefather blood, on the root.

I spent my whole adult life seeking out MOUFS, and now I must be one. What am I but a Mouf without a cock? The all in seeking of pleasure. No thrusting. I am an orifice. A wound for He. Her.

Sex for me now will be for me to overcome the shock of the scar, the missing along the Pubic. The hair thrusting out, and then nothing. Just tufts of skin that used to be my testicles.

Stranger: Nice place. Do you have anything to drink?
(Coat off. Onto a chair.)

Me: I have beer, well I have High Life, and some Rum.

Stranger: I will take the High Life. Can you put it over ice?

Me: Ice?

Stranger: Yes, I like it that way.
(Boots off.)

Me: To each his own.
(I fill two glasses with ice and beer)

We sit.

Stranger: How long were you staring at me before I noticed?

Me: (laughing) About 20 minutes. You seemed to be pretty engrossed in the flat screen.

Stranger: No, I saw you. I wanted to see how long you would just stare at me that intently. I felt like we were fucking.

Me: Not possible. You weren't looking back. But let's try it now and see if we can stare at each other long enough to get off.

Stranger: BORING. I would just end up grabbing you.

(Silence.)

Me: I would have just walked up and kissed you, but I thought that might not work in my favor.

Stranger: I probably would not have minded. Although it may have seemed strange with you being a girl and all. Girls are usually not the aggressor.

Me: You do realize…

Stranger: Put your MOUF on me.

The zipper is pulled, my face is buried amongst the coarse pubic hair, the blonde of it makes my nose itch. There's the tongue, and then his hand at the back of my head, steady, not holding me to task, but in power nonetheless.

I am flooded with images of my hand behind a woman's head, the supposed gentle prodding. Take it deeper, choke my member. Let it become your throat. The condescension of the act. I choke him, careful to gather the wet of my MOUF, to make the sounds of liking it.

The ummmms.
The slurps.

He comes in 13 strokes, and finished on my chin because I cannot catch it all. He does not wipe up, just zips, and takes his beer to the head. Asks if I have another, I go to the bathroom, spit and rinse my MOUF. His cum tastes tart and bitter. It is the consistency of snot. I bring him his beer, with ice and sit opposite on a small chair. The street lights dim to the coming dawn. Rest now.

CUSHMERE is making eggs. I am making paper airplanes. It's been three days since I left the hospital. In another 7 I will have the final staples and stitches removed.

Cushmere: So man, how you feeling? They give you any good drugs? You know how hard it is to get blood out of hardwood. Man, there was blood everywhere. I was sure you were dead. Part of me thought Damn, Bob done finally lost it and shot a crack-head in his own apartment! They got any leads as to who...?

> I was silent, and Cush put a plate of burnt eggs in my face.

Me: How do you burn eggs?

Cush: Well damn, I didn't know you was expecting Betty-fuck-ing-Crocker.

Me: You are black and somehow, by some cultural magic, you cannot make scrambled eggs. What kind of misanthrope are you?

Cush: The only kind you like. I'm gonna roll one. You want your own?

Me: Naw, I may hit yours.

Cush: I don't want you hitting mine, hence, do you want one?

Me: Oh.

Cush: I have the right not to share a joint with my best friend.

Me: So true. Love the self-determinism.

Cush: Did you see they caught the ring-leader in the Dyson Assassination?

Me: Yeah. He was some type of environmental activist right?

Cush: NO. He was a government agent because Brother Dyson was speaking to power.

Me: That's funny.
>	I do not realize that Cush does not find that nearly as funny.

Cush: Shit man, he was murdered by the State. Ain't nothing funny about it.

Me: Yeah, I guess. It seems to me that they would murder someone a bit more important if it was a political hit.

Cush: And who would that be?

Me: Shit man, I don't know, its not the 60s. I mean, what do we really have to bitch about?

Cush: You are just fucking with me, right? The fucking drug laws for one, the lack of higher education for minority students for two.

Me: Minority students? Dude, you are drinking the kook-aid.

Cush: Well I gotta get going, lots of kook-aid to drink.

Me: Man, come on. I'm just joshing you. You don't have to go.

Cush: Listen. I know you are in a dark place, but open your eyes man, we, WE are in trouble.

Me: I know...

Cush: Hey man, take care of yourself. I will give you a shout later.

I watch him walk up the block, gone in the shuffle he has employed since I've known him. He is upright, steps measured. Purposeful, no longer a deer caught, no longer prey.

I'm drifting along the outer banks of the downtown. Cigs dangle, no destination, no purpose. It's funny because so much of my day centered around my cock. I never thought of it before, but it was the leader. What it needed, the validation it required. The little protests when I would get too wasted to allow its fill. I chased a nut, I chased a high. I chased a line, a word. Text toward a beautiful collapse.

I was coming in the arms of a beer. I was the shunner of intimacy. Runner. It would always be true. I was a coward in the midst of the shiny things. My cock trying to reach out, touch the sweet envelope, the MOUF of it, her lips perched just so along my groin. Each of us dying in the learned roles. The questions never entering. Out of mind, empty heart. I was coming in the arms of a beer, of a fuck. And she loved me. Full ebony hair, the raven whisper of the chill blue, the eye clutch of the tiny. And she would grind at my wall, demand to be seen, demand a present. There I was in beauty. Between the envelope thrusting with average meat like it was holy.

Ten strokes.
Twenty. The pulse of pubic bone, and the sweet whisper: *'I love you'*.

I kept walking up the hill, out to W. 6th, crossing at Terminal. The park benches at the Veterans Memorial, pigeons dance along the litter. The true citizens of this dying CITI.

Moldy Dread: Hey man, my man. You got a quarter?

I give him two.

Moldy Dread: You got a cig?

I give him one.

I give myself one.

Moldy Dread: Ain't seen you around here, what ya' doing? Now if you ain't looking for talk, I understand, not everybody want to chat. Some folks just want keep it all in. You know?

We smoke. He lays out on a bench, a dozen plastic bags strewn like ghosts around him. I wonder if he names them.

Moldy Dread: You got a lot of demons, man. I can see 'em, over ya' head. They throwing down on you bro, real tough ya' dig?

I say nothing to this. The memorial fills up. Families, other bums. Teens. Each in their own way dying CITI. I am no longer the Man. My banishment, my wandering. I've become the no thing.

CITI.

WHEN you look up, the money towers, skyscrapers phallic the sky, a few birds, then the den of traffic, the dizzy. We are perfect in our innovation, but it is this that kills us. We bristle against the modern, some of us fall gutter, never to get back up, and those of us lucky enough to make it die the same. Alone. Tucked as a memory in the colored paper of a snapshot, in the subverting eye of a reflecting, and again that is it, memory.

She is from Before, Before. The haze of crimes too old to master, the cuts of neglect. We move on, we keep going. The nagging things of what we have done stop, and cease to hold sway.

Before, Before. We were young, and in love. We were building a life based on assumptions, the what we are meant to do. She never looked away from me. She demanded that I be there, be there in that moment.
Scenes flick.

We are laying in the tall grass, near her parents' cabin. The air is nip, but we are warm, on our backs whispering secrets like children. The nagging thought of this being temporary pushed aside, for she looked at me, through me, with eyes so pure, so hopeful, that catching breath was difficult. She had no concept of that power she had, or she did, and she was a puppet master. Dangling her father, dangling me, dangling the adolescent lovers without a second thought. Perhaps the magic that maimed me is the magic that made me.

Her: Do you know what I love about this place?

Me: No.

Her: It's still untouched by our need to mean something. It's just land, just air, and open sky. I could live here.

Me: How would we eat? Where would we work?

Her: Why does that even matter? Of course we would figure it out, but that shouldn't be the first thing you think about.

Me: I love that about you.

Her: Do you, baby? Just settle your mind, and look up. Like really look. Do you see it?

Me: What am I looking for?

Her: The possible.

And she kisses me, the nibble, and the full. Full like a thousand kisses. Her tiny hands holding my face, her breath… the sweet warm of …the collapsing flash, and then

Boom. A second louder Boom.

and the ringing. Ears shredded by fear. The breaking of sound.

I'm looking up, the buildings are like swords, each one in salute for salute's sake. Smoke, the screams. Sirens. The metal tears, the stone, now pebbles. Rocks to dust.

I awake with my face on the cool bathroom tile. I lay there, a trace of dust in the seams, the rim of dirt at the bottom of the sink well.

I gather the bottles around the room, I find my underwear, I stand under the shower head till the water looses all shape and steam. I air dry on the couch, leaving a wet imprint of me, the shape I forget. This room is my prison. I do not trust myself outside anymore.

At a corner styled cafe, sipping a green tea with about four fingers of Bourbon in it, and this kid comes up, his face ruddy from sun, and beer.

Kid: Mister. Mister, you ever been told you look like Suge Knight?
        I give him my best whither look.
Me: You ever been told to fuck off?

Kid Ruddy: See, folks are just not friendly anymore. The whole concept is lost now with our mobile devices and our selfies. I know, you are just minding your own business, right? What's your business?

Me: I kill red faced nosey mothafuckas.

Kid Ruddy: See you got a sense of humor? Name is Tom, what's yours?

        Silence.

Kid Ruddy: Okay, I get it. Not the chatty type right?

Me: You wouldn't believe it if I told, perhaps it is all breaking down, and we are just pixels, a simulation of life. A means to a larger end? Perhaps neither of us is here, and we are imagining what happened in the far gone. How we interacted before the Boom, before the tumbling?

Kid Ruddy: Shit man, that's deep. So what do I represent?

Me: You represent denial. (I give him a tooth smile)

Kid Ruddy: And you?

Me: Me? I'm just a cold bucket of water. See we think of ourselves as good, as needed in a world that has no true meaning. The things in this world needs that has no true meaning. The things this world needs are destroyed, wastefully I might add, by the very thing it does not need.

Kid Ruddy: And what was that?

Me: Us. The world does not need, and never will need us.

Kid Ruddy: But... I mean ...shit man, that makes no sense, of course the world needs us. Look, who made all this?

Me: But red, how does the world need all of this? Our innovation is a function of our need to make things convenient. We consider it our domain. Let me ask you, would the world cease to exist if there were no Citis? No buildings, no cars or trains, or buses, or bikes?
(Kid Ruddy starts to lather)
Would the world cease to exist if there were no guns, or bombs? No hate? Everything that we have claimed to invent actually has proven to be bad for us as we have evolved. We were careless with the balance, we bought into the Judeo-Christian logic that we were made in God's image, and even in our lack of faith we still clung to the idea, because it gave meaning, gave us purpose. Made us believe that we held dominion over the land, the beast, the fowl.

Kid Ruddy: Well, we are sentient beings, so that should be our natural place. What else are we supposed to be doing?

Me: As sentients, we should be able to understand harmony a bit more, don't you think? We've lost all sense of balance. Just now you assumed it was your right to engage me, your sense of self depends on coming across as friendly, a citizen of the world. The more enlightened of us, the us who can interact with any community, no matter what.

Kid Ruddy: Of course it is important to be able to move in the world in a humane way, is it not?

Me: And who defines what that is? But alas, you are not real. You are a trope, a way to get to the other side of a philosophical question. The story is just cover. The intent is hidden within that ordered disguise. I can make a turn here, and you would be gone, this is my world, and you do not exist, you are not needed. The point is made.

Kid Ruddy: . . . . .

Me: NO. I will not give you anymore words.

The skull and brain caked along the sidewalk, a mosaic of not mattering. It was beyond a dust. It was a killing, a wiping out, or rub.

```
W    E    A    R    E    T    H    E
F    A    I    L    I    N    G
T    H    I    N    G    S
```

.

I'm looking for something, way past the tall grass. The emptiness of fate. I'm looking for the end, instead I am given replay.

Her: You think you know what it's like to wait here for you, to sit and miss you and worry that what I thought I saw in you was not real, that we never were meant toward forever? You hide and you sneak. You try and get past the ugliness of wanting, and what does that get you?

Me: What does any of that even mean? Since when did it become so dramatic? I'm looking for something, don't you get that?

Her: And ignoring what is here, what is present. With you it's always more, the need for more. You look, and then you mourn what you lose in the process.

Me: How can I lose what I don't have? I don't have you unless I find what I'm searching so hard for. Don't you see its all tied together? I want to matter.

Her: But you do, and does that even get you? What is it about mattering? To who? To what end? What is mattering enough, a little, to me? You matter to me.

Me: Of course, but it's not the same. Damn you for trying to make me out to be some type of egomaniac.

Her: I'm not doing anything to you, I'm just a mirror. You created me as a foil, you never bothered with asking the right questions, never bother with me real. It's just an exercise. You are practicing making. That is all. You wish for a nut, you wish for glory. You see no value in being, in the intimacy of the heat of us. You want to be a part of history? Well, what If I told you that because of you, this whole world would end, it would end like nightmares do, you sweating. Disoriented. Alone. Left out. In tatters, no voice. What if I told you the search that you were on would mean the end of it all?

Me: What the fuck are you talking about?

Her: I'm talking about mattering, that's what you want, right? You want to matter, to have some sort of godly record of you being? Well, there it is, I'm telling you the very thing you covet, that has always been your image of a good life, I'm telling you it will cost all of us. Everyone on this planet will suffer for you.

Me: You mocking me? Who does that? You speak of love, and spew hate. You whistle it long and deep. I'm not interested in the destruction of us, or any of it. You took it from me, you say I asked you to, and now it's gone. What does that leave me with?

Her: You begged for this. It was your bass. And look at you, I tell you that you will bring about the end of the world, your search, your manhood, erect, and shiny buildings, your innovation. The domain of you. And you bring up your cock. Simple-minded, weak. What will you have? What do you have? Your Mouf, your Hands, a Citi, the shiny testament of your patriarchy. But it sits on you, and chokes out everything you hold dear, everything you think to need, to love. Me. The search? You lay up, throwing your nut like stones, the boy of you.

I am watching her hold a child, the skin is blood orange, the light from the window hides the face just above the eye, the child does not squint, there is never a blink. The child is beyond solid, present. I will melt into walls rather than hold you. For to touch this child will me the Before, Before. The tall grass. The BOOM.

It is enough that we are together, in this, playing out the designs, holding true to scripts intent, as the amateur actors. I've been here Before, Before. And she says it will all fall because of my need to matter. It's my right, I mean, this is what we are put here to do, in the striving we make our way, the order of it.

The narrative is shrinking.

FINISH,

(OR THE BLOOD THAT LED.)

Corner play, she is standing cowboy-legged against the boarded store-front, her Mouf slightly open, she is popping gum like an expert. You never see the gum, or teeth, just the slight gap, pulling you in, eyes brown, dull pennies. The prize coin in new piggy banks. Events conspire, and even through all of this, the lines against her mouth are drawn weary. Her skin has grayed through the waiting. It is not remarkable, but available. They are the 2 dimensions of a Cock-full life, the ways and cobble to it—the patriarch shudders for the public display is not in keeping with the code. We are the invisible predators. We are the shadowed things. The veneer of polish, the Jesus and oh sweet tuck of Mama.

Gray Cowboy: I see you hawking, keep walking.

> A smile plays on my face, the face of the man who hides.
> When I look in the mirror I tend to keep it masked
> the silent, sullen boy. Blank face.

> I walk a bit past gray, and call back
> "You got some time for me?"

Gray Cowboy: Piss off, I'm not working.

Me: You are not working, ok, and I'm the Easter Bunny. Sure.

Gray Cowboy: You got to be able to muster a better line for yourself. Ain't you a writer?

Me: No. The narrative is shrinking. I'm not in command.

Gray Cowboy: That's not what I asked, but oh well, it happens. Sometimes we swing for the fences and whiff Tee-ball style, you know?

Me: Yeah. Question remains. Do you have any time?

Gray Cowboy: I'm looking at you, you are not of this time. Makes me nervous, wondering exactly why you seem so intent on staying here.

Me: Really? That's a strange statement to make, even for a crack-head.

Gray Cowboy's face changes, and the change shines like tea candles.

Gray Cowboy: What makes you think I'm not an angel? You were religious once upon a time, right? Surely you've heard the story of the leper?

Me: You are mixing religious stories, this is a simple transaction. I give you money, you put me in your Mouf, you fake like you mean it, and I cum, and then smell like sixteen dirty ashtrays. Repeat. Rinse. Repeat. Rinse. Sooner than later you pick the wrong man, and you end up in some alley, your head split open, pussy torn to shreds. They try heroic measures, but pronounce you dead on arrival. Jane Doe, 23 years.

Gray Cowboy: You missed one fine detail.
Then she smiles and the light goes out.
Me: Yeah. Ok. What did I forget?

Gray Cowboy: Well, come to think about it, you missed a few things, but I will start with the one. It will be your murder. The murder you called for Before, Before. You will be a killer. In fact, it has already happened.
Gray Cowboy walks ahead, toward the back of the crumbling storefront, and points.
Gray Cowboy: See? The second thing you missed was this.

It was then that I saw the blood and flesh around her Mouf.

The intense white, searing back of my head. I look down and blood is soaking the front of my pants. Someone else screams, it's choked from afar, muffled silencer of a gun. The weapon, my weapon is in between her teeth. The corpse floats above us, and dissolves into rain.

Gray Cowboy's voice floats out of the drops, thicker, slower than before, but her.

"I got time if you will answer this."

She is now back where it all started. I stammer back against the brick.

"Okay"

Gray Cowboy: Why would you pay for what the woman, your woman, will give you for free?

Me: She is not mine.

Gray Cowboy: Bullshit. I'm not either... you a liar. Of course she is. She has chosen you, in spite of it all. She is yours because she deems it so.

Me: That's too simple. Much too simple.

Gray Cowboy: There you go, not taking ownership of the pages. Why must you pretend to not be in full control?

Me: What? Don't pretend to understand. If I was in control, as you say, why would I allow myself to suffer so?

Gray Cowboy: There's a word for that, but you won't give it to me. And there's the rub, you think you are suffering.

Me - OF COURSE. You were right here, were you not? You saw... well you saw yourself, dead, floating in the air... and

Gray Cowboy: You seem confused. We've been talking for only five minutes. Nothing has happened. But you still haven't answered my question.

Me: She is a mother. She is the mother of my children. I ...
Gray Cowboy: You?

Me: I wish for strangers. I do not want to know anyone, for anyone to know me. I want to be free to change, change faster than I can within knowing. Knowing does not adapt.

Gray Cowboy: Hence the characters trope and revolt against you.

Me: I call bullshit, lets assume the characters in a work could revolt, why would they decide to be a trope? That's not something any good, self-loving character would do.

Gray Cowboy: What does mattering have to do with imagination? It always comes down to that for you, eh?

Me: So? We already been through this.

Gray Cowboy: Yes, but you still haven't answered my question.

Me: Of course I did. I wish for strangers.

Gray Cowboy: Suppose I gave you two options.
Option #2 would look like this:

> one act in your whole life can be taken away if you would just allow for me to wipe the area of mattering out of your mind.

Option #1 would be like this:

> you can choose to be another person, you can actually say I want to be _____   _____
> and it would happen. The You, You are would never exist. Which option would you take?

Me: Easy. The first one. The first option is the best.

Gray Cowboy:Wait, Option #1 is the best, or the second thing I said is the best?

Me: I don't know, shit. Well… Option one.

Gray Cowboy: So be it.

Me: Wait, that's not what I mean. I meant the first one.

Gray Cowboy: Yes, the first option. Cool. Well, face the wall and we can get started.

Me: Is this going to hurt?

Gray Cowboy: NO, of course not. You are such a coward. Turn around.

> I turn around and face the wall, my hands up against the brick. I can feel brick dust slide into my fingerprints, my hands start to lose sensation, the falling asleep. There is a crack, the sound of a wooden bat striking the ball in the sweet center. The sound comes apart like millions of atoms splitting, shredding themselves against assumption. The telling of a Me in CITI.

The hints before Her cut me.

The things we decide to unravel.

The push when we do nothing.

Beyond an ear for suffering,

We do not know anything.

Gray Cowboy is whispering against the dense splitting of atoms:

"You will now commit a murder. The rub is that
I am not a victim.

I am a Christ sacrifice to paint the picture of a gone."

The whole of My Me ached like a battlefield, the aftermath smolder was present in my face. My Mouf was cracked by wind, and this wind was long ago, my wound had become a separate mouth turned on its side. I gathered spit, only to fail, for water had left me some time ago.

Had there been a Citi here? Wrapped up in the phallic promise of towering stone. The omen omni of erect. Always the fucking position of a top. The sky a giant womb wishing me.

LAWS OF THE STREET

Addicted To Love

Vol. 2

Written by Lamont Carey

Edited by
C. Labbe
Sharon Coker

Book design and graphics Created by
J. P. Lago

Photo of Lamont Carey taken by

LAWS Of The STREET. Vol. 2

Twitter: @lamontcarey
Facebook: LaCareyentertainment,llc/ lamontcarey
Distributed Worldwide
ISBN-13: 978-1-945806-06-3

Special thanks

Pharaoh, Joshua, Elijah, Phillip, Khalil, Libra Mayo, Robert & Ella Carey, Tracy Carey, Christine Ingram, T. Brooks, Mark Holden, Holli Holiday, Jenny Kim, Susan "Lady Flava", Sharon Coker, Brenda Richardson, Bianca "Mz. B" Brown, T. Brooks, CL, Lisa Lindsey, Carrie, Jermaine Ingram, Lil Tye, Bunmi Love, Jessica Stull, Hermond Palmer, Michelle Bowman, The Laws Of The STREET Cast and Crew, and to all the individuals who have supported my work by encouraging me to live my dreams. Special shoutout to the men and women in jails and prisons around the world that write to me to encourage me. You started this journey for me. The dream is real!

"Keep Your Hustle but Change Your Product!"

Dear Reader,

I want to tell you that everything you want you can own. If you want to write a book, start writing. If you want to start a business, start it. If you want to be free, work towards it. Everything is possible!

You deserve your life to be exactly how you want it. Just know, you may have to put in a lot of work to get it. You may have to survive a lot of no's, but you're already built for the outside rejections and challenges. It's your internal voices, fears and hesitations that tell you that you're not good enough. You're aren't; you're great enough!

I've started my journey behind prison bars. You could be starting your journey from a worse place. I do not care where you start, just start. Once you start, you will be further ahead than you were yesterday, even if you can't see it.

I just want to tell you that you're worth it. You're worth the life you want for yourself. Go grab it!

Sincerely,

Lamont Carey
Author

CHAPTER 1

The clear night sky is calm as it hovers above Washington, DC. Light traffic zips up and down both sides of Interstate 295 that passes the Benning Road Exit. On one side of the interstate is the Benning Road Subway System where a mixture of impatient and relaxed people waits on the subway platform for their trains and on the opposite side is a small church and Lucky Seven, a 24-hour convenience store. Positioned on the opposite side of the street behind the store are two huge low-income apartment complexes. One complex is named The Fair and the other complex is The Dwellings Apartments. Both complexes are three stories high with four apartments on each floor. They each have thousands of African American residents. The Fair has a black metal gate around the whole complex. The gate resembles prison bars, but without the barbed wires running across the top. There is unrestricted access to The Dwellings Apartments. Across the street from The Fair are new single-family homes and a middle school. The school has a small parking lot that can park twenty cars.

The lights inside of The Fair complex are dim. It is hard to make out a person's face if they are not within twenty feet of you. Low visibility is not good in a drug-infested community. There are always people trying to get to one place or another or to one thing or another. Each building has its own parking lot behind it with a huge trash container big enough for the residents' garbage. The parking lots are even darker. Some of the parking lot lights have been smashed or have been shot out to reduce visibility even more.

15 year old Crud is inside one of the parking lots. He is a short and a muscular teenager with a low haircut. He is seated on the asphalt with his back against the trash can in the back of his building. The upper half of his shirt, arms, and chin are covered in blood. His head is lowered in deep remorse as he cradles Little Man's dead body in his arms. Chunks of blood are visible in the scalp of the dead 250 pound 15 year old with long and thick dreadlocks plastered against his and Crud's body.

"They are back there!" A woman screams from one of the windows.

Detectives Anderson, High, Jenkins, Malls, and Flowers cautiously approach the area with their guns drawn. They train their guns on Crud when they notice Little

Man's body and the gun near Crud. They surround him.

"*Crud, put your arms in the air now. Crud? Crud, I need you to move away from the weapon now!*" Detective Anderson demands.

Crud looks up slowly at him with eyes that seem to have been crying his whole life. Anderson immediately lowers his weapon. "*Is that Little Man?*" He whispers with compassion.

Crud nods his head slowly as his eyes begin to tear up. Then he looks down at his dead friend and shakes him gently. "*He won't wake up.*" He says in the most innocent and childlike voice.

Then Detective Flowers steps up beside Detective Anderson with her gun aimed at Crud's head. "*Crud, I need you to move away from the weapon now!!!"* There is no compassion in her voice or body language.

Detective Anderson signals her to stop. She reluctantly stops. *"Crud, what happened?"* Detective Anderson says with parental concern.

"He won't wake up. Please don't die. I am sorry." Crud whines.

"Was this an accident, Crud? We will understand." Detective Anderson says with a comforting tone.

"I didn't do this. I wouldn't do this. Can you wake him up please, Detective Anderson?" Crud pleads as he looks up into the man's eyes.

"*Who did it, Crud? Did he kill himself?*" Detective Anderson questions.

Crud slowly shakes his head as he looks down at his friend. "*No, he wouldn't do that.*"

"*Whose gun is that Crud?*" Detective Anderson questions.

Crud looks down at the gun. "*It's his.*"

"*Can I help him, Crud? We need to get him to the hospital. Will you allow us to do that?*" Detective Anderson says as he cautiously takes a step forward.

Crud nods in agreement. Then Detective Anderson walks over and kicks the gun away from Crud and Detective Mall quickly retrieves the gun.

CHAPTER 2

Five o'clock in the morning, 15 year old Angel walks out of her apartment into the hallway. She is average height, slim, very pretty with shoulder length hair that is tied in a plait at the back of her head. She has on sweatpants. She stops mid-stride up the first step, she spots her mother, Praise, slouched over against the wall. Praise is extremely sick. Dope-fiend sick. She painfully stares at her daughter and forces a smile. Despite her sickness she is still a beautiful short woman with a long ponytail. The two of them resemble one another. "*Look at my baby. It's 6 o'clock in the morning and you about to go get that money, right, Baby?*"

Angel sighs as she stops before her mother. "*I got to make sure we eat…. Where were you last night? Why didn't you come home? You know Faith was sick and Divine wouldn't go to sleep because he wanted to see you. You know you're our mother. I am not the mother."* Angel says with pleading frustration.

Praise frowns with a look of agony as she rubs her stomach. *"Come on, Angel; I don't want to hear this. Mommy is sick. I need you to make mommy feel betta. You got me right, Baby?"*

Angel frowns. Then she digs down in her sweatpants and pulls out a large Ziploc bag filled with bundles of heroin. Her mother perks up and starts dancing in place. *"You know how to take care of mommy…Hey, ya youngsters don't know nothing about this dance here. Do ya, Baby?"*

Angel holds the bag in her hand. She just stares at her. Then Praise stops dancing. *"What's wrong?"*

"Ma." Angel pleads.

"Don't start that, Angel. Mommy is sick right now. I'm goin in a program. You know I am. I just need time to get things in order. You know I need to make sho' you, Faith, and your brother Divine will be taken care of while I am gone. It's coming together. Just give me some time."

"But Ma'..."

Not now, Angel. I have to talk to some people today about getting me in the program; that's why I came to you, so mommy won't have to be sick when she goes in there. You don't want them to take y'all away from me, right?"

Angel lowers her head in defeat. Then she retrieves a bundle of the drugs from inside of the bag and hands them to her mother. Praise holds the bags to her nose as if she received a blessing and starts dancing once again. *"This still Tombstone, right, Baby?"*

Angel pouts with a look of regret, *"Yes, Ma'am."*

Her mother starts laughing and does another dance move. Then she quickly kisses her on the cheek. *"Yeah, yeah, yeah…Baby, you know Mommy loves you. When I come out the program, I'm going to get a good job. Then you can stop selling this shit. We going to get us a nice place in the suburbs. We going to be living in a very*

nice place. We going to have fun like we used to before this shit." Praise promises as she angrily shakes the drugs in her hand.

"Faith and Divine will be glad to see you." Angel says with a tone of a 5 year old as she looks down instead of in her mother's eyes.

"I will go see them after I take care of my business about this program. Take them to school for me again today." She says before leaning over and kissing Angel on the cheek. *"You be careful out there today. I saw the jump-outs on Minnesota Ave. I heard one of those young guys got killed last night".*

CHAPTER 3

Slim is crossing the street through early morning traffic. He is a slender 26 year old with a regular haircut. He walks up to a group of pay phones outside of a convenience store on the corner and grabs one of the phone receivers. He was shocked to see that one has a dial tone. He inserts some coins into it and dials a phone number.

O.G. rolls over in bed and grabs the ringing cellphone on the nightstand. He is a 53 year old, tall, slim man that wears cheap round prescription eyeglasses except his glasses are lying on the nightstand where he retrieved the phone. Rachel rolls over and faces him. He sits up as he places the receiver to his ear and caresses her forehead.

"*Hello?*" He says with his barely awake voice.

She grabs his hand and smells his palm before kissing it. She is a 40 year old white woman with long blonde hair and sparkling blue eyes.

"*Man, this labor shit sent me on this job that's paying $35 for fucking eight damn hours! Then I get here, and they want me to set up some heavy ass car parts… for a fucking exhibit! I'm talking about a whole motherfucking engine! Not broke down. Not missing parts. I mean the whole shabam. They wanted me to carry this shit up four flights of fucking stairs for $35 fucking dollars, O.G. and they got a fucking crackhead helping me!*"

"*Man, what time is it?*" O.G. asks.

"6:30 in the morning. Then O.G. I had to be at the damn place by 5 in the morning! Man, they are only paying me $35 motherfucking dollars! I'm not joking. When I saw that damn engine, I rolled out."

"So what are you going to do?" O.G. calmly says.

"I left!" Slim replies.

"I already told you that the white man doesn't have your best interest at heart. Look, I have to get around the way to get some of this money, meet me around there." O.G. replies.

"R-ight." Slim replies.

Then O.G. hangs up the phone. He looks down at Rachel and smiles.

CHAPTER 4

The street is quiet with no foot traffic except for a few residents heading out to go to work. Mostly newer model cars are parked along the street of this beautiful single-family community. Then Madness walks out of one of the homes and gets in Light Skin's double-parked car. Madness is a slim, 17 year old, baldheaded, medium height teenager with a caramel complexion. He is wearing his extremely dark sunglasses.

"What in the fuck is wrong with you?" Light Skin says in anger. He is a 28 year old dark-skinned man with a bouncer frame. He's not muscular or fat. He is 5'10" with sparkling white teeth.

"What?" Madness responds with a look of confusion.

"Why did you kill that kid, Madness? Why in the fuck you never think!"

"Light Skin, you told me to persuade Crud but don't touch him."

"How does that translate into kill Little Man? Why couldn't that mean what I meant? I meant for you to talk to Crud!"

"Man, I'm a motherfucking Killa. That's what I do. That's all I do. That's what you pay me to do. So why do you expect something different from me?" He sincerely responds with a look of confusion.

"You're right. From now on, I'm going to make myself as clear as possible. So do we need to stop by the cemetery?"

Madness nods his head as he reclines in the seat. Then Light Skin holds out his open palm toward him and aggressively wiggles his finger at him. Madness sighs. Then he pulls out the gun he used to kill Little Man with from his hip and hands it to him.

Light Skin shakes his head in disappointment as he places the gun under his seat.

Madness reclines in the seat and stares out the window as Light Skin drives off, shaking his head in disappointment.

CHAPTER 5

A bird struts across the windowpane on the outside of the apartment. It stops and looks directly into the bedroom at Crud.

Crud is lying in the center of his bed in a fetal position with the white sheet covering his whole body, except for his head. He is rocking and whimpering. Then he pulls the sheet over his head and continues to rock and whine.

The bird starts strutting in the direction it came before flying away.

CHAPTER 6

The sunlight peeps through a slit in the closed living room curtains. The room is otherwise dim. Aunt Charlene is fully dressed. She is seated on the couch with her head down and her hands covering her ears. Her brother is towering over her and trying to comfort her by rubbing her back. On the floor in between her feet is a framed picture of Little Man smiling, a Kleenex box, and balled up Kleenex tissues scattered around the floor.

"Aahhhhhhhhhhhhhhh! Little Mannnnnnnnnnn! Noooooooooooo!"

The man quickly grabs for her as she collapses.

CHAPTER 7

There are patches of drug dealers and users scattered around the area. Angel is making a drug sale and her 15 year old boyish looking friend, Toni, is being her look out. Tye is making a drug sale. He keeps looking around for the cops. Tye is a light-skinned, short 15 year old with an average build with light mustache and a welcoming smile and laugh but today he is serious.

Berry comes happily up the street. He is a skinny, dark-skin, average height, 17 year old with half-a-inch plaits all around his head. He throws a few punches at an unsuspecting addict, Dirty, but misses. He laughs and strolls over to Tye as he continues to make his drug transaction. He throws a few punches at

Tye that Tye immediately moves away from and frowns at him as he counts the

money the junkie just handed him. He immediately confronts the junkie, "*Youngin, you owe me a dollar or give my shit back.*"

Berry walks up and invades Dirty's personal space and stares menacingly at him. Dirty looks frightened. "*Let me owe you a dollar, Tye. You know I am good for it.*"

"*Fuck dat. That could be lawyer money. Give dat shit back before I beat yo ass. Woop. woop.*" Berry demands with a smile.

"*I have some change. I don't think it's a dollar. I'm sick, Tye.*" Dirty pleads before turning his back to them and ruffling through his pockets and pulls out some change. It is close to a dollar. *"This is all I got."*

Tye takes the change before balding up his fist like he is considering punching the man in the face. *"Man, that looks like 75 cents. You need another quarter to get my shit."*

"Tye. You rather lose $9.75 over a quarter? You're a petty dude. Woop. Woop." Berry says laughing.

"Come on, Tye. You know I'll pay you a quarter." The junkie pleads.

"...yeah, Awright. I want my fucking quarter." Tye says seriously to the man as he stares threateningly into his eyes. Berry shakes his head in disbelief. Dirty smiles and walks off. Then Little Bible Study walks up to them.

"What's up, Baby Jesus. They said the Lord rose early but damn 7am in the morning. Woop. Woop." Berry says jokingly to the 17 year old teen with braids and tattoos on his arms and neck. Berry and Tye burst into laughter. Little Bible Study does not find it funny. *"Hee-hee. I am surprised to find you two sinners so cheerful."*

"It's the joy of having your holihoodness in our presence. I think I'm catching the Holy Ghost. Woop. Woop" Berry jokes. As Tye laughs and Berry spins around in a circle, making his eyes roll in the back of his head. Little Bible Study is starting to get irritated.

"So, I take it that it's not true?" Little Bible Study says through clenched teeth.

28

Berry stops and looks at him. "*What?*"

"*That somebody smashed Little Man last night?*" Little Bible Study replies as he watches their eyes.

Their smiles fade as Tye steps forward, "*What? Naw. Ain't nothing like that happen. We would know about That.*" Tye replies.

Berry signals Angle to come to them. She does with Toni in tow. "*Woop. Woop. Say it again.*" Berry encourages him.

"*I was told the police found Little Man's body in the alley last night.*" Little Bible Study says as he scans their faces.

"*Wh-at?*" Angel says with a look of horror.

"*What time? Because we were together late last night. Woop. Woop.*" With a look that says, you're lying, Angel gives.

"*Around 1 or 2.*" Little Bible Study replies.

Berry whips out his cell phone and turns his back to them. He starts dialing Little Man's phone number. Tye steps up beside him.

Angel runs off. Toni starts strutting behind her before taking off running to keep pace with her.

CHAPTER 8

Crud is still deeply saddened and depressed. He slouches as he walks to his front door in his boxer shorts and T-shirt. He opens the door, and 16 year old Keyonna is standing there with a look of deep depression. She is dressed very stylish with her bright yellow outfit and white see-through shirt and carrying a yellow book bag to match. She just stands in the doorway looking at him. *"Where is he, Crud?"*

He reaches his hand out to her. *"Come in."*

She takes his hand and steps cautiously into the apartment. She releases his hand. Then she plants her back against the wall by the door. He lowers his head with a look of sadness.

She begins to cry. "*Tell me the truth. Is he…?*"

Crud nods his head confirming. She slouches down to her knees and buries her head in her hands. She cries. He stoops before her and gently rubs her knee and says, "*I'm sorry.*"

She shoves his hand away and quickly pops up. She wipes her eyes and stares angrily at him. He stands. "*Crud, what did you get him into? What happened?*"

"*I don't know. You know I wouldn't do nothing to get him hurt! That's my damn best friend.*" He says, crying. He quickly turns his head and wipes his eyes dry.

She hugs him around his neck. *"I'm sorry. I know. I know, Crud."*

He hugs her and begins to cry with his face buried in her shoulder. She caresses the back of his head. *"It hurts so bad. Everybody is going to blame me but this ain't my fault. I wouldn't do that to him. You're his girl, you should know this."*

She grabs him by his head and look into his eyes. *"Crud, do you know what happened?"* Keyonna asks.

"Bodies would be dropping if I knew. But I'm going to find out. Watch me. And I'ma take care of it. Right now, I just have to get all of this stuff out of here before the cops come. Then I'll find out what happened". Crud replies.

"*Give me the stuff. I'll drop it off at my house before I go to school.*" Keyonna says.

He nods his head sadly in agreement. Then he swiftly walks to the back room and returns with a stuffed gym bag. He hands her the bag. It is heavier than she anticipated. He stares into her eyes, "*Thank you.*"

She smiles and caresses his cheek. "*It's going to be ok. Did you tell his aunt?*"

"*I gave the cops her number.*"

She starts crying hard, "*I can't believe he is gone.*"

Crud hugs her and kisses her on the side of her head.

There is a knock at the door. They step apart from each other. She wipes her tears away as he opens the door. Berry and Tye are standing in the doorway. They look at Keyonna then immediately glare at Crud with suspicion as she lowers her head and walks out without speaking to them. They wait until she walks down a few of the steps before Berry steps toward Crud.

"Where is Little Man?" Berry questions sternly.

Crud smirks before slumping against the wall and burying his head in his palms.

CHAPTER 9

Earl is reclined in his seat behind the steering wheel of the car. He is a tall, slinky, 21 year old with a medium complexion and short plaits. Vanessa leans over from the passenger's seat and kisses him on the lips. She is a 15 year old high school girl with braces and glasses. After kissing him, she grabs her backpack off the floor of the passenger seat. Rob is leaning way back into the backseat of the car and shielding his face with the hood of his hoodie from the view of pedestrians. He is a 19 year old, short and stalky teenager with a high yellow complexion and a quirky voice.

"Do you need any lunch money?" Earl questions.

Vanessa smiles as she shakes her head no.

"*Call me later on tonight. I want to see you, ok.*" Earl states.

She nods her head in agreement as she smiles at him. Then she waves to Rob. Rob smirks. She exits the car. A few school kids can be seen walking past the car to the school building. She leans over the seat and kisses him again.

"*Go on to school, Girl; before you get me started. Call me.*" Earl states.

"*I love you. I wanna go with you. I don't want to go to school today.*" Vanessa replies.

Earl frowns at her, "*NO. Bye.*"

Vanessa smirks then closes the car door as she pouts and walks off.

"Your ass is going to end up on how to catch a predator." Robs says in a serious tone. Earl burst into laughter.

CHAPTER 10

Angel leads her 10 year old sister, Faith, and 8 year old brother, Divine, up the sidewalk. She looks as if she has been crying. Her siblings are carrying backpacks and Divine has a lunchbox. Other school kids are walking around them.

"She's going to fall!!!" 10 year old Jaden playfully shouts from within the crowd of children laughing. Finally, Angel sees who the kids are taunting. It's her mother Praise. The children are crowded around her. Praise is standing with her knees bent and leaning over as if she is going to fall, but she doesn't. Her body just stays in that position. Her eyes are closed, and she starts nodding in a Heroin high.

Angel burst through the crowd of children and stops in front of her mother,

"*Ma!*" She screams. The taunting kids stare at her in shock. Faith walks through the crowd but stops at the edge of them and folds her arms across her chest. She stares in anger at her mother. Divine trails behind but stops next to their mother. Angel gently shakes her mother's shoulder.

"*Ma, what are you doing?*" Angel whines with a look of regret and embarrassment.

Praise eyes slowly open. She smiles at Angel and weakly rubs the girl's cheek before nodding back off. "*Baby, that's some good shit you gave me.*" Praise mumbles.

Divine tugs at his mother's shirt, "*Ma!*" Then he wraps his arms around her. She snaps upward and rubs his face before robotically rubbing him on the top of his head. She leans forward but not close enough to kiss him on the top of his head.

Her lips still go through the motions. She slowly caresses the top of his head, still nodding with her eyes closed. *"This is my baby boy right here. Where are you going, Baby?"*

"To school, Mommy." He says.

"Where is your sista Faith?" She says with her eyes barely open.

He points over to Faith. She is still standing off. She looks pissed off.

"She's right there." He says.

"That's your mother, Faith?" Jaden says with a condemning tone.

"*No! That is not my mother! My mother is dead.*" Faith barks before she storms off.

Angel looks sadly at Faith before she starts walking after her. Her mother continues to nod. Divine grabs and holds his mother's hand as he stares after his sisters.

CHAPTER 11

The police precinct's parking lot is full of police cars, motorcycles, other police vehicles and gas pumps. Detectives Flowers, Jenkins, and Mall are standing around their two unmarked police jump-out cars. They are talking. Detective High is seated sideways in one of the cars with his hand on the open door. They are all dressed in civilian clothing except with police insignia on their arms and bullet proof vests. They each have on their issued police belt with gun holster or leg strap, gun, mace, and handcuffs. Their badges dangle from their necks.

"So, I start teaching math when I punch out today." Detective Mall states.

"*You're wasting your time. If they wanted an education, they would have stayed their asses in school.*" Detective Jenkins replies in his deep voice.

"*Then again that may be a great idea. By working with the school, you will know who they are when we need to find them.*" Detective Flowers replies in her soft and excited voice. She and Detective Jenkins giggle.

Detective High stands and looks at his vibrating cellular phone. "*I thought you wanted to be a gangster rapper?*" He says sarcastically.

"*Why don't ya believe that they want a better life?*" Detective Mall.

Detective Anderson swiftly walks out of the building waving some folded papers.

"Lets go kids! We have the search warrant!" He says moving swiftly to one of the cars.

Detective Jenkins and Flowers high five each other before all the officers' jump into the two unmarked cars.

CHAPTER 12

Angel walks around the corner and sees her mother with her forehead pressed against the fence. She is still high off heroin. Angel struts over to her and pokes her with her finger. *"You're a liar! You don't care about us! YOU DON'T CARE ABOUT US!"*

Praise's eyes struggle to open and slowly looks at the girl without taking her head off the fence. Then her hands slowly move up and grab the fence. She finds enough strength to push herself upright. She immediately starts nodding off. *"Angel?"*

"Look at you! You don't care about anyone but yourself! What kind of mother

are you," Angel says in anger, but more pleadingly.

Toni and Snowflake are walking up the street from the opposite direction of Angel. They are dressed for school. Snowflake is a 15 year old short, full-figured but shapely, and pretty white girl with a huge smile.

"I'm your mother. Don't talk like that to me. I deserve respect." Praise demands with the slowest movement her body could make.

"For what!!! For being a junkie!" Angel screams. Toni walks over and reaches out to Angel, but Angel aggressively jerks her shoulder away. Snowflake just stands there.

Praise slowly wipes her dry mouth as if saliva was running. *"I am your junkie! You give me this shit!"* Praise says with hatred.

"Yea so you won't sell my body again to feed your habit! I hate You!" Angel cries.

Toni wraps her arms around Angel. Snowflake walks up and rubs the back of the girl's shoulder as she whines. Her mother starts nodding again.

CHAPTER 13

Light Skin gets in behind the wheel of his sports truck with a newspaper in his hand. He hands the newspaper over to Madness on the passenger seat.

"Did I make the paper again?" Madness says with a smooth tone and a hint of excitement.

"You always make the paper." He says casually; then his tone turns into anger. *"I really hope you're not showing this shit off to people! This is nothing to be bragging about. And I don't care about that shit. So don't take pride in it! This one was wrong. You killed that kid for nothing!! Are you listening?"* Light Skin says angrily.

Madness leans back in his seat. *"Yeah, I heard you."*

"*See if you can find that article about the crack laws being retroactive. When you find it, read it to me while I drive.We have to go show our respects to Little Crud and to see if he had a change of heart*".

Madness flips open the newspaper as Light Skin puts the truck in reverse.

CHAPTER 14

M.T. is standing in front of his Rasta female drug-connect who is standing in the doorway of an almost vacant house. Spliff is a 26 year old, slim built, dark-skinned female with thick, soft plaits that resemble dreads but are not and are soft and shiny looking. Her sidekick, Beauty, is also 26 year old with a smooth caramel skin tone, short curly hair and a swimmer's figure but a round butt. Spliff is always smiling but Beauty never smiles. M.T. hands Spliff a duffle bag. Then she points to a treasure chest in the corner.

"200 pounds of marijuana and 6 kilos of cocaine." She says with her thick Jamaican accent.

She then hands the duffle bag to Beauty as M.T. walks toward the chest with his arms stretched out as if he awaits the treasure to run to him. Beauty drops the bag and rumbles her hand through the stacks of money inside.

CHAPTER 15

The passenger window of Light Skin's truck rolls down. Madness sees Crud being led by Detectives Jenkins and Detective Flowers to the backseat of an unmarked car. Crud is not handcuffed. Detective Anderson is talking to Detective High who is carrying what appears to be evidence in large trash bags and shoe boxes.

Madness and Crud lock eyes as Detective Jenkins shoves Crud's head inside of the backseat. Madness nods his head with a look of anger. He rolls the window up, hisses and rubs his knees.

CHAPTER 16

Dawn walks toward Slim from the hospital. The parking lot is huge. She is wearing her nurse uniform. He is seated on the hood of her car smiling.

"This is a surprise." She says smiling. Dawn is a 26 year old voluptuous brown skin woman with dreamy eyes and dazzling smile.

"I miss you." He says smiling back. He stands and hugs her. He playfully leans her on the hood of her car and dry humps her. She quickly tries to shove him off her as she scans the area with a look of discomfort. But she can't break his hold.
"Boy, I am at work. Stop. Get off of me." She demands.

He laughs before releasing her.

"I thought you were going to that labor place I told you about?" She says with skepticism.

"I did. It didn't work out. Look, you can't get me a janitor job or something here? Fuck, I'll even be a nurse." He says half-jokingly.

"Don't play…they are not going to hire you. I already told you this." She says firmly.

He smirks as he leans against the car. She tries to comfort him by rubbing the side of his cheek. He moves his head away from her hand.

"You'll find a job. Did you check into the Employment Services?" She says with hope.

"I did that shit three months ago when I first came home. All they have is construction type of shit." He replies.

"Something is better than nothing. You don't have to work there for the rest of your life. It's temporary." She speaks.

"I went. I went out on the jobs that they sent me to. Motherfuckers acting like I'm not trying. I don't know how to do this shit! Plus, I have a fucking record." He says in frustration.

"You will find something. Look, you have a record, so you have to look extra hard, and you have to prove yourself. You *should go get a trade like I told you* *when we first met."*

"And what is that going to do, make *my record go away."* He says with sarcasm.

"It's your fault that you have a *record."* She says sternly.

He frowns at her before walking off.

CHAPTER 17

Angel comes strutting out the door behind another group of twelfth grade students. She is carrying two thick schoolbooks in her hand. She doesn't notice Toni leaning against the wall waiting on her. Angel briskly walks down the steps as Toni comes off the wall. Snowflake walks hurriedly out of the exit doors and doesn't notice Toni. She tries to catch up with Angel.

"Angel! Angel, wait up." Snowflake hollers.

Angel looks back without stopping and sees both of her friends coming towards her. *"I have to get home!"* She says with urgency.

They stop within a few feet away from her.

"Is everything ok?" Toni says.

"You fat ass white bitch!" Vanessa screams in southern drawl. She is a 15 year old, short teenager with a girly figure, braces, and shoulder length hair.

Snowflake spins around on her feet and starts charging toward the girl. Vanessa is standing in the middle of the steps with two of her girlfriends, Jackie, and Lady behind her. Jackie is a slim 15 year old with burgundy and blonde weave that hangs down to her waist, clear nails with a lot of gloss lipstick. Lady is a full-figured 16 year old with form fitting clothes on.

Vanessa tosses her books down. Toni grabs Snowflake by the arm. Angel stops and turns around.

"*Get off of me, Toni! I'ma beat this bitch ass!*" Snowflake screams back.

Vanessa jumps off the steps and throws her hands in a fighting stance. "*Come on, Whore! You ain't black for real, Bitch!*"

"*I'ma whip your ass though! Ima whip your ass though! Toni, let me go!*" Snowflake screams.

"*No.*" Toni says calmly.

Vanessa swiftly moves toward Snowflake. Toni holds out her hand to signal Vanessa not to keep coming but she does. Snowflake is doing her best to break free. Before Vanessa can get close enough to swing, Angel drops her books and steps in front of her. Vanessa stops and they stare into each other's eyes.

"*We don't have time for this.*" Angel says agitated.

"*This doesn't have shit to do with you! I told that bitch don't even speak to my man! I guess I have to beat her white ass to make it clearer.*" Vanessa replies.

"*Let me go!!! Let me go!!*" Snowflake screams, still trying to break free from Toni.

"*Then maybe your man is the problem.*" Angel boldly says.

Vanessa looks shocked, "*Bitch, your dyke ass don't want it. You can get it too!*"

Vanessa says, focusing on her eyes as she leans back and balls her fist.

Toni steps in between them and stares threateningly into Vanessa's eyes.

"*The ambulance wouldn't arrive in time.*" Toni calmly threatens.

Immediately Snowflake breaks free and hits Vanessa with a flurry of punches. Both groups clash into a fistfight. Angel is instantly hit and falls to the ground.

Security quickly jumps in and starts snatching them up.

CHAPTER 18

Berry looks sad and withdrawn. He pulls the backpack off his shoulder and digs into. He pulls out 2 DVD movies and hand them to the man standing in front of him.

"Yeah, that's it right there. Woop. Woop. That's that new action flick starring John Boy and this one is a cartoon the kids are going crazy about. Woop. Woop."

M.T. pulls up and parks. He climbs out of the car and walks in Berry's direction. He has a jacket on and zipped up.

"Are they clear?" The DVD customer questions.

"*Come on, Man. Woop. Woop. We gotta go through this every time? You know my shit is clear. You won't see no moving heads or nothing.*"

M.T. disregards the man and steps up to Berry and they embrace. M.T. looks dismissively at the man and nods his head towards him. "*We're talking.*" M.T. says.

"*Excuse me?*" The DVD customer says with a look of irritation.

M.T. bulks up and steps to the man. "*Do you have any idea who I am?*"

Berry spreads them apart. "*Woop. Woop. Chill, M.T. Let me get this money.*"

"*That's your problem. You keep chasing this little money. I'ma stop wasting my time with you shopping bag carriers."* M.T. says sarcastically.

"Man, how much do I owe you?" The DVD customer says as he turns his back to M.T.

"$20 or you can get three for $25. Woop. Woop." Berry replies.

The man hands him a $20 bill. He mugs M.T. and M.T. grins. *"You live around here?"* M.T. says as he steps in the man's space.

Berry quickly shakes the man's hand and pulls M.T. away.

"Berry, this isn't a good reflection on my business with you selling this bootleg

shit. I have an image to uphold." M.T. says with cockiness.

"What I suppose to do…stay broke until you decide to front me something? Woop. Woop." Berry replies.

M.T. turns his back to the street and retrieves a pound of marijuana from inside his jacket. Berry drops it inside his book bag. He zips the bag up. "When you stop being a welfare baby and start buying, you get it sooner. I'm doing this from the warmth of my heart. This shit actually slows my money down. But I like you and I want to make sure you become something, Shawty." M.T. says as he holds out his hand. Berry shakes it. "Call me when you have my money." M.T. says as he walks off.

CHAPTER 19

Principal Douglas is seated behind her desk and writing on a form. Toni is standing in front of the desk with her hands behind her back and staring down at the front of the desk. She is trying her best to look sorry, but her body language reads dismissive.

"*You leave me with no choice. And you do not seem to care whether you are suspended or not. So, young lady, you will be expelled for two weeks and a meeting with your parents will decide whether you continue to attend this school.*" Principal Douglas says before flinging her hand forward with the paper in it. "*I will see you in two weeks, Young Lady. Make sure your guardian is with you. And If I may suggest, I am sure the way you dress is the cause of many of your problems. I advise you to return to school if you are allowed back in here, dressing and acting like a decent young woman. Good day.* Send your friend Mary Ann in."

Toni sighs heavily before turning, snatching the door open and exiting the room.

CHAPTER 20

Crud is seated in a metal chair asleep with the side of his face and open palms on the metal interrogation table. Detective Jenkins walks into the room and eases the door closed behind him. Crud looks up. Then he sits up. He is exhausted.

"Can I go now?"

Detective Jenkins walks slowly over to the table and leans in front of him. *"You haven't helped us out, Crud."*

"I don't know nothing." Crud replies.

"That isn't what the streets are telling us. I heard about what you did. I also heard Little Man didn't appreciate that. So, I'm saying…if your road dog doesn't have

your back, you had to dump them shells in his ass. I understand that. Those are the laws of the streets. I just don't understand why you want to play games with me. When are you going to fucking be a man and take responsibility for yo shit?" Detective Jenkins says.

"*You don't even suppose to be talking to me. I'm a minor. My mother isn't here, nor have you respected my rights to a lawyer.*" Crud says as he sits up and looks more alert.

Detective Jenkins smiles and nods his head. Detective High peeps in.

"*TV is a motherfucker.*" Detective Jenkins replies, shaking his head.

"*Do you need me?*" Detective High says.

"*Yeah, he doesn't know what that wall feels like.*" Detective Jenkins says as he steps away from Crud. Detective High storms into the room and snatches Crud out of the chair, slams, and pins him to the wall. Detective Jenkins jumps in the boy's face.

CHAPTER 21

Angel is seated outside of Principal Douglas' office in the middle of a row of chairs against the wall. She has a scratch on the right side of her mouth. She looks at the clock and it reads: 1:30pm. She pouts and slams her back against the chair while folding her arms across her chest.

CHAPTER 22

Snowflake is seated in the chair in front of the principal's desk. She has a bruise on her left cheek and a scratch on her nose. She is looking up as the principal towers over top of her. "*That sounds like reverse racism, and I feel intimidated. Are you a racist, Principal Douglas?*" Snowflakes sarcastically demands.

The principal angrily slams her knuckles on her hips and frowns down on the child. Then she goes and snatches the form off the desk, scribbles her signature on it, and jams it in Snowflake's hand. "*Get out now! Two weeks. Not one day sooner. And I want to meet with your parents…Get out! NOW!*"

CHAPTER 23

Crud's mother, Ericka stops her gold sports truck in front of Crud's building. She is a very attractive 33 year old woman with big eyes and a butt that is even bigger. She dresses like a teenager. Crud looks withdrawn and heart-broken in the passenger seat. She reaches over and caresses his cheek. *"You okay, Baby?"*

He nods his head in agreement. She smooths down his eyebrow with her thumb as she looks in the rearview mirror before looking at him. *"Are you sure? Would you like for me to spend the night with you?"*

"Naw. I'm okay." He replies looking out of the window. He looks over at her as he reaches for the door latch. She gently grabs his arm. He looks over at her.

"*Are you going to be able to maintain the rent by yourself?*" Erica asks.

Crud nods his head in agreement. Then he exits the car.

CHAPTER 24

Principal Douglas has her chair at the front of the desk next to Angel. She is holding Angel's hand in hers as she stares at her. Angel is looking down at her knees. Her cheeks are wet from crying.

"You are such a sweet girl. You'll be graduating this year, head of your class. Do you realize what kind of position this puts me in? I don't want to expel you. You have so much potential, just tell me, Angel, who started the fight?"

"I honestly do not know. When I came out of the building, I saw my friends fighting. I tried to break it up, but the guards grabbed me too. I didn't do

anything wrong." Angel whines as she looks and sees that the clock reads 2pm.

The principal pats the back of the girl's hand with her free hand. *"I know you didn't start the fight, but you were involved. It is not your place to break up altercations. This is why we have security. I want to believe you and I do but I have to suspend you for three days."*

"Three days! Principal…" Angel whines.

The principal reaches over, signs the form, and hands it to her. *"Please do not complain. I gave the other girls two weeks. You can go to your teachers and get the assignments so you can study while you are suspended. I want you to consider changing your friends. Those two are headed nowhere fast and they are willing to take you with them."*

"Yes, ma'am. Can I go now? I have to pick up my brother and sister from school and it is going to take me a half-hour to get there on the bus." Angel says with sorrow.

The principal nods.

CHAPTER 25

Crud is walking up the steps toward the front door of his building. He stops in the middle of the steps, holds his arms out on both rails, and stares over at the police crime scene tape that is blocking off the alley area where Little Man was murdered. Then he looks up to see a well-dressed man in business attire with a briefcase staring angrily at him. The man gestures toward Crud's arms that are blocking his passage.

"My fault." Crud quickly and respectively moves out of the man's way.

The man stares menacingly into his eyes and shakes his head with a look of disgust as he passes him. Crud watches him with a look of interest. Then he enters the building. He goes up the stairs to his apartment and unlocks the door. He goes to close it, but Aunt Charlene slams her hand onto the door to prevent it from closing. He locks eyes with her and sees pure hatred. He lowers his head with a look of shame as he steps back. She steps half way into his apartment.

"*I bet you didn't expect to see me!*" She barks.

"*No, Ma'am.*" Crud replies.

She threateningly points her finger at him, "*You killed my nephew.*"

Crud looks baffled. "*What?*"

"*I don't know if you pulled the trigger, yet, but I am going to make you pay. You fucked up. You messed with the wrong family.*" Aunt Charlene says.

"*You wrong.*" Crud says respectfully.

"*Ok...well, who did it?*" She says sarcastically.

He lowers his eyes. "*I don't know.*"

She steps up into his face. "*I'm going to make you suffer since I can't kill you.*"

"*Check this out. The only reason I haven't spit in your motherfucking face is because you're his aunt, but, Bitch, don't push it.*" He says with rage in his eyes.

She shakes her head with a look that says, "*You just fucked up*". She turns and walks out of the apartment.

CHAPTER 26

There are junkies and other people shopping or hanging out in the area. O.G. and Slim are standing in the middle of the shopping center talking. Mrs. Janice and her best friend Mrs. Ruth drive into the parking lot and park. Mrs. Janice is driving.

"Is that your boy standing over there? You know this where they sell that dope? You didn't tell me he was selling dope again, Girl." Mrs. Ruth says in her squeaky high-pitched voice. She is a pudgy, short, light-skinned, senior with prescription glasses and short stylish red hair.

Mrs. Janice swiftly gets out of her car. Mrs. Ruth is climbing out of the passenger seat.

"*You back on the block I see!!*" Mrs. Janice says.

Most of the people in the area freeze as if their mother or the police were talking to them.

"*Shit.*" Slim mumbled under his breath.

"*And it is about to hit the fan.*" O.G. says in fear. He starts walking off. He waves to Mrs. Janice as she swiftly walks towards Slim, her son. Mrs. Ruth is right behind her.

"*Don't speak to me…ever again!*" Mrs. Janice says with hatred to O.G.

"*He ain't nothing but the devil! He got your boy back out here already. Knowing you trying to raise him right."* Mrs. Ruth instigates.

"Ma'?" Slim says in an embarrassing tone that says, get your friend, as he stares at Mrs. Ruth.

O.G. disappears into a store as Mrs. Janice and Mrs. Ruth surround Slim.

"Don't Ma' me! What are you doing?" Mrs. Janice demands with her hands on her hips.

"Nothing." Slim mumbles with a defeated look.

"That ain't what they do around here. You selling dope! Don't be lying to your mother. We're no fools." Mrs. Ruth rages.

Mrs. Janice looks at her friend. *"Let me talk to my son."* She says calmly to her friend.

Mrs. Ruth disappointedly folds her arms across her chest and pats her foot on the ground. Mrs. Janice gestures for the woman to move on.

"Well. I'm going on into the store." Then she walks toward the same store O.G. entered.

Donny exits the store and holds the door open for her to enter. Then he stops and watches Mrs. Janice and Slim.

"Ma', I know how this looks but I ain't doing nothing." Slim replies.

"You don't have a bag in your hand from the store. This is a drug-infested area

*and you are a former d-r-u-g dealer.
What do I suppose to think?"* Mrs. Janice
says calmly.

"*You suppose to believe what I tell
you.*" Slim says looking innocently into her
eyes.

She frowns as if she has a nasty
taste in her mouth. "*Ok. Well, I want you to
stay away from that O.G., O.B. or whatever
his name is or move out of my house
immediately.*" She says then she walks off.

CHAPTER 27

M.T.'s truck is parked underneath the night sky on a narrow street of single family homes. M.T. is seated behind the steering wheel counting money. Rob is seated in the passenger seat watching Earl talking to Vanessa. He can't hear them because the window is up, and rap music is playing softly. She is seated under the stop light and near the back of M.T.'s truck. Earl is stooped in front of her with the truck facing his back. One of his feet is on the curb and the other in the street.

"*Vanessa, I'm not trying to hear this! How is it my fault?*" He says with irritation. Then he stands and leans hard on the truck making a thumping sound inside.

M.T. immediately rolls the driver's window down. *"Hey! Get the fuck off my truck!!!*

He gets off the truck and helps her up. *"I'm a take care of that. You know it's only you. Nothing coming between us."* He says before kissing her on her forehead. She looks at him like he is crazy. He smiles and kisses her on her lips and waves her to the house. He watches her go into the house. He climbs in the truck and M.T. drives off. She calls him immediately. He reclines in the backseat and talks to her. When they get a few blocks away, he tells M.T. to pull over because he spots Snowflake walking down the street with a bag of carryout food. He gets out of the car. The engine remains running with the music playing.

"*Vanessa, call me back.*" He hangs up the phone and reaches for Snowflake arm as she tries to walk by him. She pulls away but stops. "*Don't touch me!*" She barks.

"*Why you tripping on me?*" He says in his most seductive voice as he continues to try to block her path every time, she tries to pass him.

"*You need to learn how to handle your hoes? I am tired of beating bitches asses over their stupid ass men.*"

"*Why you disrespecting me?*" He says with irritation.

She stops and stares up at him, "*Because I am probably about to be put* out of another school. And for what, some dick that I don't even want."

He blushes and tries to rub her hair. "*Oh, you don't want none of this now?*"

"*You want me, not the other way around.*" She says firmly.

"*Fuck you. You hear me? Fuck you.*" He says threateningly.

"*Trust me, you are not. You need to start messing with women in your age group.*" Snowflake says sarcastically.

He grabs the handle of his gun that is tucked in the waist of his pants. "*Get the fuck out of here before I kill your stupid ass.*"

Snowflake places her hands on her hips and stares at him daringly. He jams the barrel of the gun against her forehead.

Her eyes tear up. "*Do it, Earl. I am not scared but watch how much time you get for killing a white girl.*"

Rob jumps out of the car. "*Man, what in the fuck are you doing?*"

M.T. gets out of the truck and cruises around to the passenger side of the car. He shakes his head in disappointment.

"*Bitch you ain't white.*" Earl barks as Rob moves the gun down to Earl's side.

She wipes her tears away and walks off.

CHAPTER 28

Faith is looking in a pot that is cooking on the stove. Angel is at the kitchen table with Divine and helping him with his homework. *"If you add two plus four together, what will that equal? Write it on this blank paper right here and add it up. Two plus four."*

He looks blankly at her.

"Do you understand? If you have these two pieces of paper right here and you add this pencil, this saltshaker, and add this pepper shaker, and this book together, how much would that add up to?" Angel says encouragingly.

He points and counts all the objects. Then his head jerks toward the front door when it opens. *"One, two, three, four, five…Mommy!"* He jumps down and runs to his mother as she closes the door behind herself.

She still looks under the influence of drugs, but she is no longer nodding. *"Hey, baby."* She welcomes his embrace.

Angel looks over to Faith. Faith rolls her eyes at her mother and continues to stir the food in the pot.

Praise leads Divine over to the table. He does not release her leg. She hugs Angel and kisses her on the side of her head. Then she holds her face steady as she looks into her eyes. *"Angel, I am so sorry about earlier. I didn't mean it. You ain't to blame for my problem. You be helping mommy out. Do you forgive me?"*

Angel looks sadly up at her and nods her acceptance. She hugs Angel again. Divine remains clenched to her leg.

Praise looks over at Faith. "*Girl, I didn't know you were in the kitchen. Come and give Mommy a hug, Faith.*"

Faith rolls her eyes. "*I have to use the bathroom.*" She says before walking into the bathroom and slamming the door shut.

Praise's bottom lip drops as she looks at Angel, "*She's still mad at me?*"

"*I'll talk to her.*" Angel replies.

"*No, I'll do it.*" Praise replies.

"*Mommy, can you help me with my homework?*" Divine says with hope.

Angels smirks and laughs.

"*Sure, baby. Do you mind, Angel?*" Praise asks.

"*No. Are you in for the night?*" Angel replies.

Praise nods her head in agreement. Angel smiles and pops up. "*Cool. I have to make a quick run. I'll be back shortly.*"

Divine hops in Angel's seat. Angel walks toward the front door.

"*Faith, I'm running out. I'll be back in a little while.*" Angel leaves and goes to Crud's building. He is seated on the living room couch and cradling Little Man's picture. He stares sadly at his friend. She knocks on his door.

"Who is it?" He shouts.

"Angel!!" Angel replies.

He lies the picture down and opens the door. She steps in. She looks at him with concern. *"I would of came up here earlier, but I had some issues to deal with. How you doing?"*

"I'm good." He says as he goes and sits on the couch. She sits beside him.

"Everybody thinks this is my fault." He speaks.

She playfully nudges him. *"You are Crud."*

He chuckles, *"I don't know how to take that. I'm glad to see you were worried about me. So does this mean I got a shot now?"* He says looking at her with desire in his eyes as he reaches out and caresses her arm.

She pulls away. *"No. boy! Don't you supposed to be in mourning?"* She forces a smile and tries to playfully dismiss his advances.

He sits closer to her and caresses both of her wrists as he stares into her eyes. *"You know how I feel about you."* He says in a soft vulnerable tone.

"*You just want some ass, and you know I don't get down like that.*" She speaks.

"*I only want some of your ass. So, is Toni blocking?*" He says sincerely.

Angel pulls away and walks out of the door. He gently grabs her by the arm. She snatches her arm away and shakes her finger in his face.

"*Don't keep grabbing on me! I'm tired of all of ya' talking about us. Whatever we're doing if we are doing anything it's our business. It's not yours or any of these people around here.*" Angel says.

"*I was joking.*" Crud replies.

"*Don't play with me like that. I have to get home.*" She says in frustration.

"*I'll walk you out.*" Crud replies as he follows her out of the building.

CHAPTER 29

Detective Anderson shuffles behind Aunt Charlene as she exits the station. She is visibly upset. *"Excuse me, Ma'am?"* Detective Anderson says.

Aunt Charlene stops in mid-stride down the stairs. She looks over her shoulder to him. He stops at the top of the stairs. *"I kind of overheard you in there. Are you a relative of the kid found in the alley last night?"*

"Yes. I am his aunt." She says as she turns around to face him. Detective Anderson extends his hand out to her as he moves closer.

"I know your nephew by Little Man." Detective Anderson replies.

She looks puzzled. She shakes his hand. Detective Jenkins walks out of the station and joins them. *"And you are?"* *Aunt* Charlene asks.

"I am Detective Anderson, and this is Detective Jenkins. We discovered your nephew's body." Detective Anderson replies.

"The kid Crud was with him." Detective Jenkins says accusingly.

"He should have been. He killed him." She snaps back.

"How do you know this?" Detective Anderson says leaning forward as if he is waiting for her to tell him a secret.

"I know it in my gut. I am going to prove it. So, what are you all going to do about it?" She says with skepticism.

"We are investigating it. You know it is hard because no one is talking to us, not even Crud. If you could tell us what you know, I will be glad to look into it. I think Crud is involved but I don't have enough to arrest him." Detective Anderson sincerely says.

"I'll get something. They'll talk to me, but can't you do something? He lives in an apartment by himself. His mother moved out to do God knows what and he keeps guns and drugs in there."

"We searched the house and didn't find anything. He's like 15, right?" Detective Jenkins replies.

"*And what does that mean? He is a menace to society.*" She glares at him.

"*No, I was saying that, because he isn't supposed to live by himself. Maybe we can get Child Protective Services involved.*" Detective Jenkins says it with a bright idea look.

"*You are dumb as you look. That will not get him convicted for killing my nephew.* Detective Anderson, *I appreciate you wanting to help but…* as she pauses and rolls her eyes at Detective Jenkins, I see I have to do this on my own." She says.

CHAPTER 30

Rob is seated in the passenger seat of M.T.'s truck and M.T. is on the driver's side.

"I'm telling you; somebody is going to kill us. M.T. We have to do something about this." Rob says.

"He's a grown ass man." M.T. says in a I don't care tone.

Rob looks out the rearview mirror and sees Earl standing at the back of the truck. He is looking for Vanessa, but she is not in view. Then he whines the window down less than an inch.

"But she's not..." Earl coos."

"*I can't do this. It is getting so hard.*" Vanessa complains.

Earl stoops down and caresses the back of her head. "*You can't drop out of school. Then what you gonna do?*"

She looks angrily up at him. "*So, you gonna leave me if I do? You gonna treat me like everybody else?*" She starts crying. *I'm tired of ya leaving me. Why can't anybody just love me. All I want is to be loved.*" Vanessa replies.

He wraps his arms around her shoulders. She turns into him and wraps her arms around him. He inhales the scent of her hair. "*Where am I going, Shawty?*" Earl asks.

CHAPTER 31

Light Skin is stopped at the corner with his left signal on. He sees Crud and Angel walking onto the walkway outside of Crud's building. They stop walking and stand about 50 feet away from the corner where Light Skin's car is stopped.

"*There goes our boy.*" Light Skin says gesturing.

Madness leans forward and looks over at him. "*That's the little dyke chic with him?*"

"*Her name is Angel.*" Light Skin says in a serious tone.

Madness opens the car door. "*I'm getting out.*"

CHAPTER 32

Dawn is seated behind the wheel of her van. Slim is on the passenger seat. She is parked in front of her building. The van is running.

"*I don't care if we have only been dating for three months. You are not getting any. I told you; I am saving myself for my husband.*" She says annoyed with his questions.

"*Shawty, you acting like you ain't never had sex before.*" Slim says irritated but not done trying.

She turns and stares into his eyes, "*I'm not sleeping with you. I told you that in the beginning.*"

He looks out of the window in frustration. Then he turns and stares seriously at her. "*So, I have to marry you to get some?*"

"*Yup.*" She says nodding her head and now looking straight ahead at her building.

He leans in toward her, smiles and caresses the top of her hand. "*Well, I'll marry your ass then.*"

She snatches her hand away and frowns at him with a look of disgust. "*Nope. What can you do for me? You don't love me. You just have a hard dick, and you want some. You are not ready to get married anyway.*"

"This is some bullshit. So, what are we doing? You said I'm not getting none and I'm not ready for marriage. What are you doing? Why you wasting yours and my time?"

"I like you, but I am not taking care of no man and I am not having casual sex. I am willing to be your friend, hangout with you and help you get yourself back on your feet, but I am not fucking you."

He leans back in the seat and exhales toward the window. He looks at his watch. *"Look, it's 9:45. I need to get home."* He says with an attitude.

"I thought we were going to have dinner at my spot. Oh, because I ain't fucking you, now you want to go home. Oh, ok." Dawn replies.

He continues to stare out of the window. *"Just take me home."* Slim says.

CHAPTER 33

Crud and Angel are still standing on the sidewalk outside of Crud's building. Angel notices Light Skin's truck pull up and double park. His driver's side window whines down.

"I heard about what happened to Little Man. You okay, Crud? Heyyyyyy, is that Angel?" Light Skin says as he opens the car door and gets out as Angel smiles at him. Light Skin walks over with his arms outstretched. Then he hugs and kisses her on the cheek. She smiles and pulls out of his arms. He reaches out to shake Crud's hand. Crud hesitates long enough for Light Skin to recognize. Then he shakes his hand. *"I'm so sorry about Little Man. I liked Shawty. Do you need anything?"*

"I'm good." Crud says dryly.

"Well, Fellus, I have to get home.
"Light Skin call me tonight. I have something for you." Angel says with a huge smile.

"I'll see you in the morning. Go and get you some rest." Light Skin genuinely says.

Angel holds her hand against her face like a telephone. *"Crud, call me if you need to talk."*

Crud nods in agreement. Then she walks off.

Light Skin looks seriously into Crud's eyes. *"Why in the fuck you take so long to shake my hand? Motherfucker, you owe me money. What's up wit' chew?"*

Madness creeps up behind Crud. With a look of uneasiness, Crud tries to step to the side. Madness follows him. Light Skin steps up closer to Crud. He is boxed in like a sandwich.

"What'cha doing, Man?" Crud says as he looks halfway around at them with a frown, but he's scared.

"The question is what in the fuck you going to do?" Light Skin says in a soft but threatening tone.

Madness whispers into Crud's ear, *"You know your man is probably lonely. You want to join him?"*

Crud tries to turn to face Madness but Light Skin grips Crud's chin. "*You're talking to me. Look, I'm going to give you this package and you're going to work that bill off. Look, I like you so what I am going to do is give you $6,000 worth of dope. You pay me 7 and we'll keep doing this until we are even. So, you're still going to walk away with 3 grand at a minimum.*"

"*Answer him. Either you wit that or we can do option two. Trust me, you don't want to do option two. So, I suggest you agree.*" Madness says with his mouth close to Crud's ear.

Crud spots Keyonna walking up the street. She is carrying the gym bag that he gave to her earlier. He becomes more macho, *"I can do that. It's fucked up but...."* Crud replies.

Light Skin puts his index finger over Crud's lips. *"Don't talk back. Take this."*

Madness reaches around Crud and presses a stuffed paper bag against his stomach. Crud takes it. Then Light Skin and Madness step back as Keyonna walks within inches of them.

She looks suspicious at Light Skin and Madness before looking at Crud with concern. *"You, okay?"*

"You're Little Man's girl, right? I am sorry to hear about your loss." Light Skin says with sympathy.

"*I need to stop at the store around the corner. Let's go.*" Madness says with no interest in her.

Light Skin and Madness start walking toward the truck. Crud grips Keyonna up aggressively by the arm as the two men get in the vehicle. "*Come on. Is all that stuff I gave you in the bag?*"

She is aggressively being pulled up the stairs. He has a look of urgency on his face. "*Yeah, I didn't open it.*" She replies, baffled.

Then he walks her up the steps.

Light Skin and Madness stares at them.

"I'll take care of that tonight." Madness says with confidence and commitment.

CHAPTER 34

Detective High is slouched down in the driver's seat of his personal car and staring at the building diagonally from him. He is parked about 200 feet from the building in the huge apartment complex. Every parking spot is almost full. A car pulls up and parks in front of the building. Pat exits the car. She is swaying her hips as she heads towards the building. She stops in her tracks and spins around. She stares directly into his eyes as he eases further down in his seat. She walks angrily over to his car. "*Roll the fucking window down!!*" She demands as she screams and angrily points at him.

He whines the window down and raises his chin at her like he was caught off guard. "*Yeah.*" He calmly replies.

"What in the fuck are you doing?" She demands with fury.

CHAPTER 35

Crud creeps along the side wall in the direction of the front of the corner stoor. He stops at the edge. He peeps around the corner to the front of the store. He sees Light Skin's truck. He notices movement in the front seat. He pulls his handgun out from the waist of his pants. He holds the gun down at his leg as he motions to take a step forward.

THE END...
TO BE CONTINUED

AUTHOR'S Questions

Can you circle your answers or email them to me at lacareymanagement@gmail.com

Could you identify who the main character's were in this book? Yes   No
Is yes, who were they_____

_____

_____

_____

_____

Could the main character's have made different decision that could have produced different outcomes? Can you explain_____

_____

What do you believe Crud is feeling as he appears in this novel ?

_____

_____

_____

What are your thoughts about Angel and her family?

_____

_____

_____

Can you relate to these character's? If yes, how so_____

_____

_____

_____

What are some the consequences of some of their actions?

_____

_____

What character would you like to see have a bigger role?

_____

_____

How do you believe they can change their lives?_____

THANKS FOR READING THE BOOK & ANSWERING THE QUESTIONS. PART THREE IS COMING SOON. YOU CAN PRE-ORDER IT NOW AND YOU WILL BE ONE OF THE FIRST TO RECEIVE!

The Laws Of The STREET Series current releases and upcoming releases:

1.   2

     The Laws Of The STREET series is about the lives, the passions, the hopes, the traumas, and the fears of a community desperately trying to succeed even if the path they choose could lead to death. This is where the odds are played, where teenagers become the head of households, where criminals set the rules and where children lose their way or find their strength. This is their truth.... behind the stories the evening news never airs. This is where accountably could lead to death.

Author Lamont Carey's prison series:

THE HILL. Follow Sherman as he begins serving his prison sentence at Lorton Correctional Compound. This complex houses some of the deadliest men in the world. It's a penitentiary so dangerous that other maximum-security prisoners don't want to go. Sherman made some bad choices in his life. Now he will either live or die from the consequences.

THE WALL is the sequel to the THE HILL. It takes you to a prison more deadly and sinister than THE HILL. Real Gangsters have been known to scream behind...THE WALL. No one is safe. There are no leaders. Everyone is a killer.

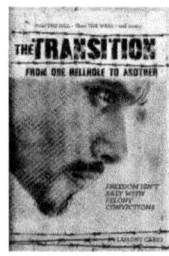

THE TRANSITION is the journey after Washington, DC's extremely violent prison system Lorton closes. Some of the prisoners are released to the community and the rest, mostly young black males, are shipped to other prisons in the Federal Bureau of Prisons (FBOP) system. Both are in for a rude awakening. Freedom isn't easy with felony convictions for those released in the community. And the federal system isn't Lorton for those transferred to the FBOP. Their new home is run by the Aryan Brotherhood who would love nothing more than to slit their throats.

Other works by Author Lamont Carey:

Dead Before 18 - Saving our boys from the Streets" is a navigational guide written to and for young boys who have and will face a complex world that demands making decisions and promises consequences. It is written from the perspective and experiences of the writer, who made many mistakes while learning how to be a man.

The goal of the book is to make these boys and young men aware of the pitfalls, so they might avoid lives of self-destruction.

Reach Into My Darkness is a collection of narrative poems that mirror the readers' very own life's experiences and barriers. The goal of the book is to inspire self-reflection, self-expression, and empowerment.

Your Art Is Your Empire is a guide for performing, recording, and spoken-word artists who want to turn their dreams into a business...and ultimately...an empire. The book covers such topics as: legal business structures, taxes, marketing, creating a bio, and creating their first product and more.

The Journal was created simply to assist you in reaching your personal and career goals. It comes complete with areas for goal setting and tasks to carry out. There are additional sections where you can journal and even draw pictures. It is great for programs and personal use.

Author/Spoken Word Artist Lamont Carey's award-winning CD containing such hits as "I Can't Read", "Confidence", "I Hate This Place", "She Says She Loves Me", and ten other electrifying spoken word pieces. Digital files are available for sale on iTunes, CD Baby, Amazon and more.

Promotional Gear - T-Shirts

Keep Your Hustle but Change Your Product

"Keep Your Hustle but Change Your Product" tee-shirt is available and advertises the difference between illegal and legal is the product. Join the movement! Order your T-shirt from the website and help spread the word!

Creative Mind

A Creative Mind Is A Goldmine. Lamont believes artist can change the world and make a living off of their creations. No more starving artist! Order your T-shirt from the website!

www.lacareyenterprises.com/clothing

Lamont Carey is an international award-winning spoken word artist, filmmaker, playwright, actor, and motivational speaker. To make booking arrangements for speaking or performance engagements for your group, students, prisoners, employees, conferences, or

at any other event you are having worldwide, contact LaCarey Enterprises, LLC:
 lacareyentertainment@yahoo.com

You may visit the website at:
www.lacareyentertainment.com

Send fan mail to:
LaCarey Entertainment, LLC P.O. Box 64256
Washington, DC 20029